The Farmer Takes a Child

*Book II of
"Charity Fish"*

Kaye M. Giuliani

Copyright © 2012 Kaye Giuliani

All rights reserved.

ISBN-10: 1477599657
ISBN-13: 978-1477599655

DEDICATION

This book is dedicated to my Husband, Gilbert Giuliani, Jr. for his unflinching support and the loving care he has always given me.

#		
1.	FIRST KILL	1
2.	ONE YEAR LATER - ON THE RUN	5
3.	IN THE BEGINNING	9
4.	OVERNIGHT	14
5.	IT'S NOT EASY BEING GREEN	18
6.	THE KISS	24
7.	TIME TO KILL	30
8.	THE CABIN	34
9.	BEFORE DAWN	38
10.	EDDIE	42
11.	MISSING, PRESUMED DEAD	45
12.	THE "WORK" END OF IT	49
13.	JANICE RULES	55
14.	OFFICER GENTRY	59
15.	JUST ME AND THE MRS.	62
16.	HARD TO LET GO	65
17.	NO HAM, PLEASE	71
18.	BILLY FISCHE	76
19.	DNA	80
20.	THE EAGER VOLUNTEER	85
21.	BARRY'S NEW DISHWASHER	87

22.	OUR HERO AND BENEFACTOR	90
23.	FREE FOOD FOR LIFE	93
24.	A FOX IN THE HENHOUSE	96
25.	CLOSING IN	99
26.	WHO DOES THAT??	104
27.	WHAT TO DO ABOUT JANICE	110
28.	RAINY DAYS AND MONDAYS	113
29.	GIVE ME THE TAPE	117
30.	IN OUT OF THE RAIN	121
31.	BILLY MEETS A GIRL	125
32.	A VOICE IN THE NIGHT	128
33.	THANK GOD FOR AFIS	131
34.	THE SHED	137
35.	CLOSING IN	142
36.	THE PADLOCK	145
37.	A LITTLE CHILD SHALL LEAD	148
38.	STAYING ALIVE	151

ACKNOWLEDGMENTS

This book would not have been possible without
the tireless support of my co-worker, Kathy Parr,
and her daughter, Kacy Thompson. They were
willing to read and comment on each chapter
as it came off the printer. As proofreaders and
cheerleaders, they were my driving force.

1. FIRST KILL

He had pulled the truck onto the shoulder just before reaching the Interstate on-ramp, making sure to park in a spot that was poorly lit and isolated. Visibility had been nil in the driving rain, and this had seemed as good a place as any to pull over and wait out the storm.

Never a bad idea to be ready for a fast getaway, either. His eyes sparkled, ominously.

Harlan's Woods grew thickly on either side of the road. This part of Fredericksburg Virginia had been home to Jack Garrett and his family throughout most of the 80's. He had smoked his first joint in these woods; gotten his first kiss, too, though that hadn't gone as well as it might have. A shadow had passed over Jack's face at the memory, and he had thrown the truck into park and killed the headlights.

Jack took in his surroundings. The trees closed their ranks against the storm. Freezing rain had sheathed every skeletal branch with an ominous black sheen, and gusting winds set limb against limb in a shadowy dance to the death.

All we're missing is the Big Bad Wolf. He chuckled.

This storm was a gift meant for him alone. It proved that what he was about to do had been pre-ordained. After all, very few people would venture out on a night like this. Jack grasped the steering wheel and savored a thrill of anticipation that started in his groin and radiated outwards to his fingers and toes. He reached under his seat and pulled out the hunting knife that his dad had given him when he was 16. It had been sharpened to a fine point, and, as he unsheathed it and slashed it through the air experimentally, the knife had actually seemed to share in his exhilaration.

Jack's intended victim had walked this trail every Thursday night for the past month; starting out at around 8:30 p.m. for her girlfriend's house and then heading home again just after 10:00 p.m. He had been watching her for a very long time. He knew where she lived, what cars her parents drove, their habits and schedules – everything he needed to know in order to make her his own tonight. Her fear of the wooded trail at night had been palpable and that had excited him. She had long brown hair that she wore pulled back at the nape of her neck. Her body had been slender, and the budding promise of breasts had given her sweater the sweetest little contour. Jack's pants tightened and saliva filled his mouth.

In the dark, it had been difficult to determine her age. Was she 14? 15? He sensed she was still an innocent -- young enough for his purpose, in any case -- and free for the taking. She was such a sweet, obedient morsel. Probably wouldn't give him any trouble at all.

Still clutching the knife, Jack checked his wristwatch. It was almost 10:00 and time to position himself for the night's festivities. He had built a makeshift blind near where the trail narrowed. If all went as planned, the child would be taken by surprise from behind, restrained, and then whisked away to a lonely thicket for "processing." He pulled up the hood of his jacket and eased out into rain, slamming and locking the door behind him. The frigid air tasted of mud and rotted tree stumps.

Little Red Riding Hood, here I come.

His forceful exhalation had hung in a mist around his face that made his transformation complete. Jack wished that his father had lived long enough to witness his metamorphosis from "Sissy Boy" to "Big Bad Wolf." As he moved silently towards his goal, the rain changed from the bright clatter of water on pavement to the softer, darker, sifting of droplets through naked limbs.

It wasn't long before he began to hear the sounds of her little feet pounding up the path towards him through the downpour. He let her pass, then burst from his hiding place to tackle her from behind. As he had rehearsed, he pulled the tie wrap from his back pocket and cinched her wrists tightly behind her before she could even catch her breath. He enjoyed being on top of her, but pulled her to her feet in a hurry to move her away from the trail and into the comparative safety of the woods. He kept the knife at her throat as he drove her forward, and it cut into her sweet neck every time that she missed a step, or tripped over debris.

"You're gonna' freeze in those wet clothes aren't ya', little girl? We're gonna' have to get you out of those and warm you up a bit. I was worried about ya'. Out here, all alone-like, dripping wet. I like's 'em wet. . . Yes, I do."

"I haven't seen your face." She whimpered, in an attempt to be brave. "You could let me go now."

"Well, of course I'm gonna' let you go! Free as a bug from a jar. I'm just tryin' to help is all. Tryin' to save the 'lady in distress.' Why, I'm your own special prince, come to sweep you off your feet."

He had kicked her feet out from under her at that point. He had taken her too quickly; killed her too soon. He scowled. But, this was only the first. He would do better next time. Make it last longer.

Her body was heavy and he was covered in blood by the time he got back to the truck. He looked both ways before pulling down the cargo gate and dropping her onto the waiting tarpaulin inside. He pulled off his shirt and added it to the macabre envelope before folding the ends around and securing it all with a length of rope.

As he drove away from Harlan's woods, he told himself again and again: *I'll do better next time.*

2. ONE YEAR LATER - ON THE RUN

Jonathan Emile Garrett, ('Jack' to anyone who wanted to stay on his good side), cut through back yards until he reached the destination that he had started for that morning; the very trail where he had taken his first 'plaything' the year before. This time, instead of being a confident stalker in search of prey, he was a fugitive on the run. The path had taken him quickly to a less-affluent community closer to the center of town. There had been a bus stop near the trail's exit where he had considered waiting for the next bus before remembering that he had no cash, coins or cards.

My fucking wallet is in my fucking truck on that fucking street surrounded by fucking cops.

He had been on his way to scope out the popular shortcut through Harlan's Woods where he had taken his first victim -- Charity Fische -- a year earlier, when things started flying around the cab of his truck and hitting him in the head and face. Shocked, he had jumped out of the truck to investigate, and something (or someone) had thrown the car into gear causing it to careen downhill into a parked car and make a spectacular noise that drew half the neighborhood out to investigate. Jack had considered hanging around to speak with the police, but knew that anyone checking his driver's license would soon be aware of his 10-year stint in prison for child molestation. If they started to put two and two together, he'd surely wind up on the top of their suspect list for the Shortcut Stalker. He didn't want to take that chance.

His only option at that point was to walk the eight or nine blocks to the shopping mall and try to catch a taxi from there to his sister's house. She still lived in Virginia, would be home today, and probably wouldn't hesitate to pay his fare. What he was going to do after that, he didn't know.

I have no keys, no identification, no cash, and no clothes. My face is going to be all over the news tonight. Fuck!

The sidewalks were bordered by identical cracker-box houses, dead shrubbery and frost-covered yards. It had been a brisk morning, and he thought it might snow. Though it had been early February, several homes still wore their shabby Christmas regalia. Poverty was depressing.

Jack wondered whether or not he could trust Eileen. Wouldn't she turn him in to the authorities when she found out what he was wanted for? What about her redneck husband and their kid? His 'activities' had been front-page news for so long that everybody across three states wanted to see him on death row.

If I killed them – killed all three of them – I could take a car, credit cards, jewelry . . .

A young couple had just driven up to one of the houses and begun to unload a toddler and some groceries. The woman eyed him, suspiciously. His heart was beating furiously as he tried to be cool and look away.

I can't kill everybody.

He tried to get control of his pulse rate; breathing in through his nose and out through his mouth the way he did at the gym. The one thing he couldn't think about – not ever – was that flattened beer can. No rational explanation could be made for what had happened that morning. He preferred to think it had been some kind of hallucination brought on by lack of sleep, indigestion or his overwhelming desire for his next 'toy.'

It wasn't a ghost. Not that girl's ghost, come to get him back for what he had done to her. Jack forced his thoughts away from that notion before it had a chance to take hold.

Perhaps he was just crazy? Weren't serial killers and rapists supposed to be a few feathers shy of a whole duck? Maybe he had been getting increasingly psychotic with each sweet child that he had been forced to destroy? All of that gory sawing and stacking. Their faces. He shuddered.

I didn't want to do that part. I never wanted to kill them. There had been no choice! It wasn't my fault. I thought they were so pretty and fresh. I would've kept them. . .would have loved them.

He tried to imagine slitting Eileen's throat and couldn't. His big sister, she had always been the one he could depend on. He could remember her reading to him when he had the chicken pox, and sticking up for him when kids called him a wimp because of his scrawny, pale body. Prison had made him what he was now; strong, muscular, nobody's patsy.

Maybe I can just tie them up and take off. Once I'm headed for parts unknown, it won't matter what they tell the cops.

Each step brought him closer to his customary calm. It was a pleasant walk, after all, and nobody was even looking for him yet. He had time. Besides, the "Shortcut Stalker" had always been able to outsmart the cops, and there was no reason to believe that he couldn't just keep on outsmarting them.

The first thing I'm going to do is cut off all this hair. Maybe dye it? Eileen dyes her hair; probably has a box or two around the house. Or, maybe I'll shave my head? I'd probably look slick with a shaved head.

He turned the last corner and headed towards the JC Penney's entrance of the local mall. It shouldn't be too hard to find a phone here. He needed to get his shit together and put some serious miles between him and this whole goddamn town. Jack's eyes glittered with predatory calm as he crossed the parking lot, and his confident strides turned heads.

3. IN THE BEGINNING

The playground at the Church of Christ in Fredericksburg, Virginia, had been ringed by 100-year-old oak trees, but boasted much more than cool sanctuary on a hot Sunday afternoon. The bright blue slide, red jungle gym, and green and white swing set beckoned to all under the age of 12. On any Sunday, swarms of three and four-year olds could be seen vying for the swings and lining up for the slide while their parents attended afternoon classes. By the time Eddie had made it through the hour-long sacrament meeting (where he was required to sit still and be quiet -- or else) he was all set to propel himself out of that building like shot from a musket, and could be seen vaulting from one item of playground equipment to another almost simultaneously.

There was nothing "quiet" or "still" about Eddie Garrett. He was a wild and loud and overactive child. The doctors called it "A-D-D with Hyper-something," and it was supposed to be a bad thing that needed pills. The pills changed color and name from time, to time, but none of them had been any match for the clanging, screeching, leaping and crashing attributes that had all worked together to make up the sum total of that boy.

Eddie's hair was strawberry-blonde on its way to red. His body was an explosion of freckles, and it had never mattered that he was shorter than most kids his age, because the parts of him that took up the most space (the loud, fidgeting, disruptive bits) had always more than made up for it. At four years of age, he was just getting ready to start school and his parents were worried.

"Is he ready? Maybe we should hold him back another year? The doctor says he may settle down as he gets older." His mother had been nursing her first cup of Saturday morning coffee with a worried crease between her brows.

"I think they meant he might grow out of it in his teens or twenties, Helen; not before he reached kindergarten."

"Well? Maybe we should consider home schooling him? I could take an evening shift at the CVS, and that would give me a chance to stay home and work with him during the day."

"We should do what Dr. Johnsen says and increase his meds enough to help him to concentrate. All of these kids are on medication of some sort or other. He's not the only one, you know." Eddie's dad had taken that moment to disappear behind his crossword puzzle. It had always been a good way to end uncomfortable conversations in the past. His sandy hair leaned towards red, but never quite made the jump. He had always been distant with Eddie; never seemed to want to play with him or answer any of his questions. Anyone watching closely would see the truth of it in a moment; he found his son unbearably obnoxious and embarrassing.

"How can that be right? He would sleep through all of his lessons and just keep falling farther and farther behind." She stirred her coffee, absentmindedly, for no reason. "The kids will be mean to him. Just think about that. They won't understand why he acts the way he does." Helen's voice took on a whiney quality that John found particularly irritating.

"Kids are always mean to each other. They always have been and they always will be. Dealing with bullies is a rite of passage. You had to do it. I had to do it. Hell, our parents probably had to do it. That's just a part of life that is unavoidable. Would you shelter him from the whole world? What good would that do him? How would he ever hold down a job? The boy needs to learn how to fend for himself."

"Still, I think it is too soon, John. He is not functioning at his age level. We should wait until he is able to keep up with the rest of the group."

Jonathan E. Garrett, Sr. put down the crossword page of the Chronicle and took his wife's hand. "He may never be able to keep up. We need to face the fact that he is never going to be like Jack and Eileen. Eddie is 'special.'"

"Oh, God; don't call him that. I hate the connotation. Eddie is just as smart as the next kid. He is just . . . socially. . . "

"Retarded?"

"No! That wasn't what I was going to say. He is just socially awkward."

Eddie had been watching the Saturday morning cartoon lineup and zooming around the family room with his assortment of cars, trucks and busses when he had stopped to listen to what his parents were saying in the kitchen. Their voices had taken on a certain edge that usually meant that something interesting was going on.

When he heard his dad say that he was "retarded," he froze beside the doorway and listened some more. Janey Franklin had called him retarded once; he had shoved her off her swing into the mud and called her retarded right back. What was 'retarded?' He wanted to know what that meant. It had to be a bad thing like the A-D-D. Were there pills for that, too?

Alerted to the sudden quiet, his mother had gone to investigate and had found him standing there just outside the kitchen door; his bright green eyes full of new questions.

"Mom? What does 'retarded' mean? Am I retarded? Do they have pills for that too?"

His mother had scooped him up in her arms — something that she didn't do much since her back had gotten hurt — and given him a big hug. "No! Of course not! You are just the most perfect little boy in the whole wide world."

"Daddy says I'm retarded." Eddie said with characteristic stubbornness.

"Daddy just used the wrong word." She had said. "Right, Daddy?"

His father had put the newspaper down with undisguised annoyance.

A man can't even do a crossword puzzle on a Saturday morning. Work hard all week and what do you get with your toast and jam? Eddie's questions; Eddie's problems and Eddie's goddamn noise. And Helen wasn't much better. Cooing and coddling the kid. What that boy needed was a couple of good whacks to his kiester.

"What have you been told about listening to people's private conversations, Eddie? Hm? Whatever I said or meant was not for your ears. I was talking to your mother." John stomped over to the fridge, pulled it open, and chugged the last of the orange juice straight from the carton.

"Ooh! You're not allowed to do that! You're s'posed to pour it into a glass. Mom? Isn't he s'posed to pour it in a glass? Dad, you're in big trouble!" Eddie wiggled loose from his mother's embrace and slid to the floor; managing to stomp her bare foot and kick her shin in the process.

"Eddie, be careful. Ouch. Go on back and watch your shows, honey. Look. You're missing Deputy Dawg."

With one more long, accusatory, look at his father, Eddie had taken off running with his arms out, airplane-style, to fake a crash landing in a lime green bean-bag chair.

"Helen, that's just what I've been talking about. You spoil that boy. He should be sent to his room with a freshly-paddled bottom for talking to me that way."

4. OVERNIGHT

Eileen was in her senior year and had dreams of traveling the world as a journalist; seeing everything firsthand and reporting it with flair. Even at 5'11", she had been proud of her height and had never slouched to pass as a shorter girl. She had thick, wavy brown hair that she kept shoulder length to make the most of its natural bounce, and she tended to toss her head when she laughed to draw attention to it.

Though Eileen loved her brothers very much, and worried about the way they were being harassed by other kids their ages, she couldn't help wishing that they would stay out of sight when she was with her friends. It just didn't look good to have two freaks for brothers. Eddie was a total "spaz" and Jack, well... Jack was... *different*.

She'd never forget her first (and only) pajama party. Her mother had promised to keep 6-year-old Eddie and 12-year-old Jack out of the house until 9:00 p.m., and then tuck them right into bed. It was only after securing her mom's solemn promise for the third time that she was able to relax and start looking forward to the arrival of her guests.

Everything had started out just fine. They had lots of food, drinks, scary movies had been rented, and all of her favorite CDs had been loaded into the player. The house, which was usually what they liked to call "casually comfortable," had been scrubbed and polished for inspection.

The girls had started to show up at around 7:00 p.m. – right on schedule, so that there had been no need to stare out the front window and pace back and forth wondering whether or not anybody was going to show. Dad had stayed upstairs in his study all night, only making one appearance to filch some brownies from the kitchen. Mom, as good as her word, had taken the boys to the movies. Everybody was running around in their best pajamas, giggling breathlessly for no reason, eating too much and having a great time. Eileen had just begun to think that she had pulled off the party of the century when she saw the headlights of her mom's Honda Civic pulling into the driveway. The boys were home.

"Okay everybody! It's time to put the movie in! Come on! Tina, Jenny, Beth? In here!" Eileen tried not to let her anxiety show as she herded all of her friends into the family room (and away from the front of the house). But, the noise level had been so high that she had only been able to gather about half of the girls before the boys had come bursting through the door.

"Awwww! I see your titty dots!!" This came from Eddie – at the top of his lungs -- as he pointed accusingly at the "dots" in question.

Eileen came around the corner just in time to see Jack gaping, open-mouthed, at Beth's body. There was something about the way he had been looking at her that gave Eileen the creeps. Quickly, she grabbed Beth by the shoulders and pulled her from view, through the kitchen and into the relative safety of the family room.

"You guys start the movie, I'll be right back."

"Eddie!" She hissed. "It isn't nice to say things like that!"

"BUT SHE WAS SHOWING ALL OF HER PRIVATE PLACES!!!" This last outburst had been so loud that Eileen had actually felt the mortification mottling her cheeks. Then, without thinking, she had slapped her six-year-old baby brother, hard, across his face.

Eddie, true to his nature, had wasted no time in dissolving into a howl of uncontrollable sobs and wrapping himself tightly around his mother's legs. Unaccustomed to receiving discipline of any kind, he had been taken completely off guard.

"Eileen Lindsey Garrett! You apologize to your brother this instant!"

"But, Mom..."

"You know he can't help himself. You are just going to have to explain that to your friends, or we will simply call their parents and send them home right this minute! And, don't even *think* about asking me to have an overnight party in this house again!"

The three-bedroom split foyer was too small for any pair of ears under the age of 110 to have missed a single word. Eileen's heart had seized up and she was pretty sure she was going to die – right then and there – but she had been forced to apologize to her spastic brother and her apoplectic mother before slinking back to join her, now subdued, guests.

Poor Beth had been so humiliated by the whole ordeal that she was now fully dressed. Try as she might to regain their spirits, her friends had voted unanimously to skip the movie and go straight to bed.

Eileen couldn't shut her eyes. She was sure that this would go down in history as the worst day in her young life, and she couldn't help playing and replaying the likely consequences of this social Armageddon.

5. IT'S NOT EASY BEING GREEN

Jack looked both ways before joining the crush of kids in the hall. It was his lunch period, but he couldn't go to the cafeteria like the rest of the kids. Nobody wanted him to sit at their table. You had to be part of a group to sit in there. Jack didn't want to be part of a group, but he would have liked to go in there today and get some pizza. Friday was pizza day. He could smell it all the way in the 6th grade science hall, which was clear across the school from the cafeteria.

So, instead of hanging a left and going towards the delicious aroma of pizza being slapped onto beige lunch trays, he was going to cross to the stairs and head for the study carrels in the library. It was against the rules to eat in there, but once you were in your own little cubby, nobody could see what you did. He went to his favorite one; second from the wall with the heating vent right above it. The rest of the school had been tiled in blue, grey and white linoleum, but the library was carpeted in a deep blue color that he found relaxing. It had looked so clean and new; probably due to the fact that very few people had ever spent time in there studying.

Jack let out a sigh. Now, he was comfortable and safe for the first (and only) time in his long school day. Nobody was around. Jack pulled a bagel with cream cheese out of his backpack, un-wrapped it, and opened his book. He always layered on the cream cheese heavily, and he loved to bite into the soft, chewy bagel and then lick up whatever cream cheese squished out the sides.

Nobody could be expected to eat with the bullies staring them down or tossing food at them. Jeez, it was hard to even breathe when you were trying to ignore all of the verbal and organic-based missiles, much less trying to enjoy a slice of school pizza.

He thought about the pizza as he chewed his bagel. School pizza didn't have any greasy meat on it, or huge globs of cheese. It was a perfect rectangle of crust, sauce and a fine sprinkle of mozzarella that had been cooked to a perfect golden brown. They usually served peas and cherry Jell-O® with it – both of which Jack would eat, but could do without.

He wondered if he would ever be good enough to eat down there with everybody else. He tried to imagine himself without the pale, white skin and the wimpy arms, the clothes that his mom had thought were "cool," when she had run across them in the K-Mart® on sale. Jack thought that he preferred being alone, but right about then he would have rather have been alone with a couple of slices of that pizza.

His mind wandered to thoughts of Angela Barnes. She had the desk right in front of him in 3rd period Math with Mr. Comus. Today, she had worn a red shirt with short sleeves and a series of little buttons down the front. Five of the seven had been undone, and her creamy skin had seemed to be calling to him. He wondered why she hadn't unbuttoned the last two, then thought that he respected her more for leaving them closed. He wanted to touch her soft, auburn curls so badly. Her hair was always there, taunting him five days a week. Sometimes she wore it up in a ponytail or braided it straight down her back. He knew she was going steady with Matthew Wallace, but he couldn't help wanting to gather all of that gorgeous, freshly-shampooed hair up and hold it to his face; smell the auburn wisps; feel the silkiness on his lips.

Most of the time, she smelled like strawberries or peaches. Her purse hung partially open on the back of her chair, and he could see the strawberry lip gloss vying for attention among the jumbled up blushes and eye shadows, foundations, mascara and bright packs of gum.

A familiar tightening in his crotch had warned Jack that this line of thought was not going to facilitate his navigation of the halls to English class, so he pushed all images of Angela out of his mind, took a big bite out of his bagel and bowed his head to read.

When the bell rang to announce the end of 4th period, Jack looked up with a start. He had become so comfortably immersed in his book that the time had passed too quickly. He gathered up his bagel wrappings and folded down the page to mark his place before shoving everything into his backpack and running a comb through his hair. As was always the case when he was forced back out into the maelstrom, his heartbeat picked up and a feeling of dread turned his stomach into a sort-of cement mixer. He tucked his shirt in, took a deep breath, and wound his way through the library's bookcases, tables and chairs before giving up the silent sanctuary by pulling the glass door open and joining the crush of inhumanity that was middle school.

"Get outta' my way, Faggot."

This time he had been able to keep his feet during impact. His decision to carry the backpack over both arms had been 'un-cool,' but had eliminated the need to scurry around under a stampede of heartless feet to recover his stuff. He hung back a bit let the owner of that assault, his arch rival, Matthew Wallace, get ahead of him, and then – without realizing it -- held his breath all the rest of the way to English in room 143.

Someday, Angela would see that Matt was just a poor excuse for a junkyard dog. She was too sweet and innocent to be with a guy like that. He pictured her creamy neck and those last two buttons; her small, round breasts, just starting to form beneath the soft red sweater. And, when she finally came to that realization, Jack would be there waiting for her; no matter how long it took.

He had been so deep in thought at that moment that he hadn't noticed the foot that had been stuck out into the aisle to trip him, and had fallen into two occupied desks before doing a face-plant on the blue, grey and white linoleum and bloodying his nose.

"Stupid Asswipe! Watch where you're going!"

"Yeah. You queer little turd-faced faggot!"

A burst of nervous laughter had come from the class members too scared of retribution to do anything else. In a situation like this, most were happy to see the target on somebody else's back.

Painful kicks came from "injured parties" on all sides until Mr. Kennedy had walked in and broken things up.

Jack was glad he had thought to carry a box of tissues. He held a wad of them under his nose and tilted his head back to the undisguised merriment of his tormentors. There was blood on his shirt, but not too much. He thought he would be able to get it out with some cold water and stain remover. Thank God there hadn't been a substitute that day. He thought they'd probably have killed him.

There it had been again. That word. "Faggot." Jack knew what it meant, but had never understood how that applied to him? He liked girls. He loved Angela. He wanted to kiss her and had never wanted to kiss another boy. Of course, he had seen himself in the mirror. He knew that he was too tall, too skinny; that his nose and ears and mouth were too big for his face and his skin was still hairless and so pale that his veins showed blue from underneath.

Any psychiatrist observing Jack's calm, logical management of this constant emotional and physical battering by his peers would have seen a ticking bomb. While he was outwardly serene and resolved to his fate, surely there must have been some dark inner voice clamoring for revenge?

Unfortunately for a great many people who would meet Jack Garrett under different circumstances, there hadn't been any mental health professionals in attendance.

6. THE KISS

When Angela signed up for chorus, Jack had decided to sign up, too. He could sing a little, at least his mother said that he could. Then they would have two classes together. Matt wouldn't be caught dead in a music class, so Jack could be certain to have her all to himself.

She mostly acted as if she didn't know he was there, but he had expected that. Most people treated him that way and he was used to it. The first few weeks the boys and girls practiced in separate groups so that they would learn their unique harmonies before coming together and hearing the final result. As awful as it had been to rehearse on the opposite side of the room, at least he had been able to watch her mouth move and enjoy the way she swept her hair behind one ear every once in a while. He thought he could hear her voice – sweet and clear – weaving in and out among the other voices, and the sound of it caused his heart to ache.

One day, he had actually brushed up against her when everyone had rushed over to pick up the music for the spring program; his right arm touching her left. For days afterward he would lay awake at night reliving that moment. He imagined the way her lips would move against his when they finally kissed for the first time. He would rehearse whole conversations in his mind – even acting out his part in front of a mirror. A couple of times he thought about asking his dad for advice, but every time he got close to saying something, his father had found some way to shoo him off. Mom would have talked with him about it, but she hadn't been feeling well for the longest time and he hadn't wanted to bother her.

In the end, it had been Eileen who had listened to his tortured tale of unrequited love. Her advice had been simple: *Tell her how you feel.* At the time it had even sounded like good advice, and he had thanked her for it. But, when was he supposed to tell Angela how he felt? During choir practice? After math class? He wrestled with that dilemma for days before coming up with a plan; then waited another two weeks before putting that plan into action.

The day before the Spring Concert, Jack gathered up all of his courage and passed a note to Angela on his way into math class. She had opened it right away, instead of waiting, as Jack had hoped that she would. A smile crossed her face before she had tucked the note away in her purse, and his heart had somersaulted and cart-wheeled and performed any number of amazing feats. For once in his lifetime, Jack allowed himself have hope.

The Spring Concert was performed on a Friday night in April. The school year was coming to an end and everyone was already making plans for summer break, so the kids had been in full voice. Mrs. Nagel had been very pleased, and her pointy face had flushed with excitement when the auditorium filled with the sound of applause.

As Jack had anticipated, Angela's boyfriend Matthew Wallace had been a "no-show" at the concert. That had meant the coast was clear. It had been easy to tell his folks that he was going to stay and help put away the risers for Mrs. Nagel, and that he would walk home later. His parents had been happy to abandon him without comment – also no surprise.

He carefully checked his hair in the bathroom mirror. He tucked in his shirt and popped two breath mints. Jack's hands were sweating profusely as he left the school and headed for the trail through Harlan's Woods. He had asked Angela to meet him there, and he was hoping with all of his being that she would show up. He stopped and put another couple of mints into his dry mouth prior to starting up the path. This was it. He was finally going to tell Angela how he felt about her. He wiped his hands on his pants, took a deep breath and concentrated on putting one foot in front of the other.

When he came to the fallen tree at the halfway point, she was there. As beautiful as any angel. So pure. So innocent. His sweet love. He gulped and took a seat next to her on the fallen tree.

"Thanks for coming." He stammered. "I have something that I want to tell you; something that I've wanted to tell you for a very long time."

"Okay." Her sweet voice was sending him over the edge. "I'm here. What did you want to tell me, Jack?"

"Well." Jack's lips were glued together. He gulped, but no saliva would flow. "I'm in love with you." There. He had said it. Then, the words just came tumbling out, unbidden.

"I've been sitting behind you in math class all year, and I just couldn't stand being so close to you every day and not being able to tell you how I felt. You are just the most beautiful girl in the universe, Angela. I haven't been able to think about anything else in the longest time. I sit awake at night wishing you were in my arms."

Angela laughed. Jack took that to mean that she was flattered by his adoration; that he might have a chance. He leaned in and gave Angela a tender kiss on the lips. No sooner had their lips parted than the forest had come alive with laughter and jeering voices. Confused and in shock, Jack had been knocked to the ground at Angela's feet.

It was Matthew and several other members of the football team. For the next five minutes they punched him and kicked him into a state of unconsciousness. When Jack finally regained his senses, it was Saturday morning. He moved one hand over his swollen face, checked the movement in his battered and bruised arms and legs, and then pulled himself painfully to his feet.

I should have expected that. I deserved it. How could I have thought that a girl like Angela would ever be interested in me. I am "a loser." Why didn't I just leave things alone? Why did I even listen to Eileen?

A leaden blackness had taken up residence his heart overnight. A shift had taken place in his psyche that was so solid and unchangeable that Jack began to view his world through a warped and darkened lens.

It was in this state of mind that he had limped home with one arm broken and his ankle swollen to almost double its normal size. There was dried blood caked around his mouth and nose, and his clothes were torn and muddied. "I look like a monster." He thought. "I am a monster." Then, when he finally reached the comparative safety of his home, his father's angry shouts had been his only welcome.

"Just where were you last night, Jack?"

"Honey, leave him alone! Look at him! He's bleeding!" Helen went to the kitchen to get a wet cloth.

"I don't give a good goddamn if the kid's bleeding. He doesn't get to wander around all night and worry his mother to death as long as I am the head of this household." John Sr. folded his arms across his barrel of a chest and fixed his eyes on Jack. "So? Where the hell were you all night? And, don't even think about lying to me."

"I. . . I. . ." Jack had looked from one parent to the other while trying to compose some kind of reply. "They. . . they. . ."

"Speak up, boy! What trouble have you gotten yourself into?"

"They were there. They jumped out. . . and. . . they. . ."

Without another word he let the buzzing darkness suck him down. His knees buckled. Jack passed out as his mother approached him with a wet rag.

The next time his eyes opened, it was in a hospital room with a cast on his arm, a wrap on his elevated ankle, and a blessed I.V. feeding pain relief through the veins of his right hand.

Though everyone tried to get to the bottom of this mystery, Jack refused to identify any of his attackers. It was probably this decision that enabled him to live to adulthood.

7. TIME TO KILL

Four days after Jack's 16th birthday, his mother died. The back pain that had been plaguing her for years had not been caused by the fact that she had been the only one "who does anything around here," as she'd thought, but by Stage IV colon cancer. From her diagnosis in early May to her death on the 5th of April, she had spent very little time awake. The pain had become so devastating towards the end that she had kept herself in a morphine haze. 10 yr. old Eddie had clung to her remaining life force with more tenacity than she had been able to. He must have sensed what was coming on some level. With mother gone, he would lose all of his defenses. He would be alone and vulnerable in a world that didn't want him.

Helen Garrett's funeral had been simple and poorly attended. A housewife with both parents long dead, and her best friend off to Georgia three years prior, Helen's life had been lived within a very small circle. The coffin had been inexpensive and unadorned (Jack's father didn't believe in wasting flowers on the dead).

Jack had approached the open casket with the intention of crying, but found that he was not able to. He had loved his mother, while he could still love, but that capacity had left him the year before, and all that he could do was wipe dry eyes and mutter a vague "goodbye" before walking away for the last time.

Eddie had been inconsolable. His sobs had dominated the brief service to such an extent that their father had actually yanked him from the room and forced him to spend the remainder of the service in the funeral parlor's hallway.

From that day on, the boys had come under the sole power and direction of their father. Even their big sister, Eileen, had deserted them by heading off to UVA in the fall. In a matter of weeks, the world had lost all of its round edges and soothing words. What followed was to be a 5-mile plummet into a dark pit lined with broken glass. The Garrett boys were in for a hard time.

Dad had never been the warm and fuzzy type. But, now that he had found himself alone in the house with his two "sissy" sons, he was on a mission. He took it upon himself to undo all of the molly-coddling and sissy-fying that their mother had heaped upon them over the years. Yep. Jack and Eddie were going to become "men" if it killed them. Jack hadn't fully grasped the threat inherent in those words until his father had come home one day with hunting rifles, knives and fatigues for each of them and announced that they were going away for two weeks to hunt deer.

Jack didn't have anything against deer. He saw them from time to time on the side of the highway or on the edge of a field, and thought they were nice. They had those soulful eyes and graceful legs. Besides, giving Eddie a loaded gun would be like dipping the Tasmanian Devil in nitro glycerin and setting him loose in a nursery school; it just didn't seem like the smartest idea.

Jack watched as Eddie took aim at the fish tank and pulled the trigger. He gulped and looked sideways at his dad.

"What's the matter? Don't you like your rifle, Jack?"

"Um. Sure." Jack's mouth was dry. He picked up his rifle and ran a hand over the shiny barrel. "Don't you think we should be shooting at targets, though? Why we gotta' kill stuff?"

"Because that's what guns are good for, son; because being a man means being able to put meat on the table when times are hard. You want to be a man, don't you, son?"

Eddie ran behind the tired brown recliner and shot an imaginary volley at the dog.

"Yeah. I guess that's okay, but you sure *he* needs to be running around with a gun?"

"What? Eddie? Oh, now you sound like your mother. Just look at him! He can't wait to get out there and start shooting."

"Actually, that's what I was worried about."

"Oh, he'll do just fine. Frankly, I have my doubts about you. Maybe I should have signed you up for a ballet class, instead? Is that it, Jackie? Would you rather be wearing tights and one of those tu-tu things and prancing all over the stage like a fairy princess?"

"No, but."

That was when Eddie snuck up and shoved the business end of his Remington Model 700 SPS compact rifle against Jack's head and yelled "BOOM! You're dead!"

All of the color drained out of Jack's face as his father stood by grinning maliciously and Eddie rolled around on the floor in paroxysms of wild laughter.

8. THE CABIN

They had unpacked all of their new gear in a cabin at Occoneechee State Park around the end of November that year. Jack's father had been in a jovial mood, and the boys had been excited to be away from home and surrounded by all of the new sights and smells. For months, the boys had been going to the local shooting range to work on their aim. Target practice had been fun, but Jack was itching to try out his skills on a real deer. Even Eddie had proven himself worthy on the shooting range. Both boys had been craving their dad's approval for as long as they could remember, and this could be just the opportunity they had been waiting for.

The two-bedroom cabin was modern and had nicer furniture and decorations than their own home. On the outside, there was a deck running the length of it, where you could stand to look at the woods and some of the other cabins. The forest smelled like dead leaves and fallen pine needles. It was a mysterious smell that invited exploration.

Jack and Eddie had their own room with twin beds. Eddie had called "dibs" on his bed before Jack had even finished getting his stuff out of the car. Everything was so clean! Since their mother had passed away, their house had been slowly losing ground in that regard. It had become a darker place, messier, and it often smelled like grease; more of a cave, really.

Jack dropped his backpack on the remaining bed and looked around. Besides the beds, there was a desk and chair, two small dressers and two bedside tables with lamps. A large painting was hanging over the desk. It showed a flock of mallard ducks rising up out of a still pond with reeds and cattails all around the edges. If you looked carefully, you could see a golden retriever's nose poking out of the reeds behind them. It was the kind of painting you could look at for a long time, because every single duck, stalk, tree and ripple on the pond had been lit by a peaceful sunrise you could see way off in the distance.

There was a bathroom right outside their door with white towels all folded up and stacked neatly on a shelf. A tiny rectangle of soap – wrapped up like Christmas -- rested in the soap dish. Everything sparkled. *Wow*. He'd forgotten what a clean bathroom looked like.

"This place is the best!" Eddie chimed as he reclined on his bed with his hands behind his head. "I think we should just move here and become hunter-guys."

"Yeah. Screw school."

They shared one of their few moments of brotherly affection. Eddie pulled his hands free and gave Jack a two-handed "thumbs up" and a smirk.

"Jack?"

"Yeah."

"Let's make the beds in the mornings and brush our teeth and stuff like Mom used to say while we're here."

"Sure."

"Jack?"

"Yes, Eddie."

"I miss Mom."

"Me too."

John, Sr. appeared in the doorway. "So? You guys all settled in? Nice digs, eh?"

"Yeah, and I thought we were s'posed to be roughin' it!"

"Ah. Well, us guys like the ladies to think we're tough hombres, but it's actually pretty cushy around here."

"Dad?" Jack sat on his bed. "Can we go fishing later?"

His father looked at the time and shook his head. "Nope. Sorry, son. It's getting late and we need to put some supper on and hit the sack. 3:00 a.m. comes early."

Both boys looked disappointed.

"We have to go to bed right after supper? Gee, Dad. We just got here! Can't we have a look around the place a bit?"

"There'll be time for that. Now, c'mon in here and help me pull some chow together. How're we gonna' shoot any deer if we're under the covers until noon? How about some beanie-weenies with rolls and butter?"

"Mmmm!"

"Sounds good to me." Jack's mouth began to water.

"Eddie. Set the table, please? The dishes are here." He opened a cabinet to the right of the fridge. "And, the silverware is in this drawer."

"Got it."

"Jack. Open these beans for me? Here's the can opener."

The old-fashioned hand-crank-style can-opener came sliding across the counter to him. "Got it."

"Just dump 'em in this casserole dish. Pull the gross chunks of fat out and throw 'em in the sink, okay?"

"Will do." Jack was still cranking the opener around the rim of the first can. It was harder than he thought it was going to be, but he was determined not to show it.

"And I. . ." His father had intoned with gravity. "I will slice up some weenies!"

"Ouch!" said Eddie, grabbing his crotch.

They had all laughed together, and it was good.

9. BEFORE DAWN

It had been pitch black in their room when their Dad had come to wake them. It had taken the boys only a moment to remember where they were and get excited about the day ahead. Jack had dressed warmly, in layers, as instructed. He pulled on some SmartWool® socks and the good hunting boots that his Dad had insisted on.

"Help." Eddie grunted; his long-sleeved tee hopelessly tangled up inside his shirt and both of them wrapped around his head and arms.

"How in hell did you get like that?"

"Oh, shut up and get me out of here!" He whined.

One of the buttons had some hair wrapped around it, and Jack could feel the strands breaking and tearing as he removed the shirt.

"Ouch! Watch it! That's my hair!"

"Okay." Jack said, handing Eddie the two – recently untangled shirts. "How about putting them on one at a time?"

"I'm in a hurry!"

"Not that much of a hurry. C'mon into the kitchen once you're dressed. Dad packed some pastries and stuff for breakfast."

"I'm coming."

"Bring your boots."

Eddie stopped mid-gallop and headed back into the room for his boots.

"Hey. You guys look good in camo." Dad said around a bite of Danish. He lifted a steaming cup of coffee to his lips and sipped.

Jack had to admit that he looked pretty tough in this outfit. It hadn't hurt that the extra layers of clothing had added some girth to his pathetically skinny frame. Eddie sat on the floor to tie up his boots. It was hard to believe he was already twelve. He was growing up so fast.

They had assembled their hunting gear the night before, and the packs sat waiting by the front door like patient shrubbery. Each "man" had signed tags, a license, a length of cord, their hunting knives, a pair of gloves, and some large plastic bags (for the internal organs – ick). Dad was carrying a gallon jug of water to use for dressing out a deer. Jack wanted to carry one, too, but Dad warned that those packs could get pretty heavy as the day wore on – even without the jug of water. Besides, the chances of getting two bucks on their first day were pretty slim. They had their rifles, of course, plenty of ammunition, and all the testosterone that each had been able to muster. Now, the game was on!

It had been hours and hours before saw their first deer. The boys were tired by then, and the novelty had more than worn off. Eddie saw it first.

"There!" He whispered excitedly.

"I see him." Dad said. "See him, Jack?"

"Yep."

"Okay. Who is taking the first shot? Jack?"

Jack pulled his rifle slowly to his shoulder and tried to get the buck in his sites the way he had been taught.

"Okay. What do you call that stance, son?"

"It's forward quarter."

"Do we take that shot?"

"No."

But, the deer lifted his head and looked around like he knew something was up. Then, he took off running; his white tail flashing and only his flanks exposed. Jack let out a breath and dropped his rifle to his side.

"Good call, Jack." He felt his father's hand on his shoulder. "Don't shoot until you have a humane shot."

"I'm next!" Eddie was too loud and it had earned him a glare.

"Okay. Eddie's up next. Stay alert, boys."

All that day and all through the next not a shot was fired. But, on the third day, there, behind a screen of dead and dying branches, stood a buck and a doe. Dad had nodded to Jack, and the rifle had been lifted. This time, the buck was broad side and the shot was perfect. Before any of them knew it, the bullet had gone home and the buck had moved off a good bit.

"Good one, Jackie! Good one! Look! You dropped him, son! You got your first buck, and a fine one he is, too!"

The doe had taken off without looking back. Jack stood where he was and watched his father walk out to examine the carcass. He felt good, but also dizzy and not looking forward to what he knew would come next; the "dressing out."

Eddie could be heard crashing through the undergrowth. He was jumping and screaming and . . . being Eddie.

Jack leaned against the nearest tree and watched them hunker around the carcass for a few minutes. *So, that's all it takes. Not as hard as people always made it out to be. The deer poses and you pull the trigger. Aim for the exit wound. A straight shot from just above the foreleg and through to the other side. He could do this. He had just proven it. Something that had been alive was now dead, and he was a hero; just as easy as that.*

"Well? You gonna' come over here and work this carcass, or you gonna' have Eddie do it for you?

"I'm coming." He called, and started for them with feigned confidence. Now he was going to have to do what they had all talked about. He'd seen pictures; watched a video. Step one, step two, and so on. He had pulled off his coat and rolled up his sleeves. The hunting knife had gleamed with innocence that one last time as he had pulled it from its sheath. The buck was shifted onto its back with its shoulders downhill. The rear legs were separated. Jack raised the knife and then lowered it to cut through the hide of the buck's midsection.

Eddie scrunched up his face in a moue of disgust, but his eyes never left the buck and no sound escaped his lips. This was a test, and they both knew it. To flinch now would be to risk everything. Father was watching.

10. EDDIE

Dad had eased up on Jack after that kill. But not Eddie: Poor Eddie. The kid didn't have a "stealthy" bone in his body. He was loud and boisterous, impatient and rash. Though he had dreamed of joining the "brotherhood" of hunters, it had soon become evident that he would never qualify. The game that he didn't manage to scare away, he would cruelly injure with a poorly-aimed shot. The injured animal would then have to be tracked for hours through dense forests before it could be humanely put down. Those were the worst times; their father moving swiftly ahead of them through the woods; wearing his furious silence like a porcupine's quills.

Jack winced at every verbal attack their father launched at Eddie over the next several months. He could see, first the hurt, and then the anger as it grew inside his brother. Day after day Eddie's manhood was called into question with particularly cruel jokes and asides. Jack wondered how much longer his brother would be able to endure it. It hadn't been long before his father had begun to physically abuse Eddie, as well.

"Dad!" Jack had come running when he heard the loud slap followed closely by Eddie's helpless whimper.

"What? Do you see anything worth defending here? This 'Momma's Boy?' Where's your Momma now, huh, boy? Whose skirts are you going to hide behind now?"

"C'mon, Dad, leave him alone. He's still a kid." Jack took a protective stance between the two of them.

"He's no kid of mine! Little wuss needs to grow a spine and become a man. Look at this report card!" The aforementioned document was crumpled and thrown at Jack's feet. "He'll never graduate at this rate. I'm not gonna' be stuck supporting him, I can tell you that! I'll put him out, first. Then, he can sell his lily white ass on the street like all the other fairies."

The front door had slammed behind him and Jack knew that Eddie had somehow managed to slip away.

"Why do you have to be so mean to him, Dad? Eddie's not gay. He's just different. He can't help it. He needs his medicine. Why won't you let him take his medicine?"

His father had only grunted derisively and stomped off, muttering obscenities under his breath.

Jack found Eddie by the creek splashing cool water on his face to wash away his shame.

"I know what we'll do." Jack said. "I'll teach you how to kill a deer better than anybody. Then, come hunting season, you'll blow him away! He'll have to stop being so hard on you, then, right?" Eddie turned a red and swollen face towards him and an odd smile pulled at the corners of his mouth. Jack wasn't sure why, but he was chilled by the sight.

11. MISSING, PRESUMED DEAD

Janice Schuster sat curled up in an overstuffed chair in front of the television, eating a bowl of Cheerios®. Her nightshirt was big enough for two girls her size, and read, "Don't Bother Me, I'm Crabby!" across the front in bold letters. A grumpy crab with a raised claw punctuated an implied threat. On her right foot she wore a purple sock, on her left, a lime green one.

Janice, like many others home from college for the summer, had not been able to find a job, so she spent lots of time in comfy clothing lounging around the house. While she found this lack of direction rather pleasant after the months of late-night cramming sessions and constant stresses of school, her mother was not pleased.

The morning news was not particularly interesting, but it would do as something to stare at while she spooned and crunched her breakfast. Then, some bold letters came across the bottom of the screen that immediately caught her attention.

"Law enforcement is searching for a young girl that went missing on Friday morning from a motel off of Interstate 64 in Charlottesville, Virginia. According to Police Department officials, at approximately 10:50 a.m., Police were dispatched to the motel after a 10-year-old girl identified as Cherie DeLapis went missing. Her mother, who recently relocated from Southern California,

reported to the officers that sometime on Thursday night Cherie walked to a nearby convenience store to buy snacks. The child never returned."

"It is believed that Cherie took this path to reach the convenience store rather than walking the long way along the main road. The overgrown vegetation could have provided cover for an unknown assailant."

"Officers have conducted a search of the motel and the surrounding area, going door to door. Cherie's information has also been entered into the National Crime Information Database."

"Cherie was last seen wearing red gym shorts and a red and white striped top. If you have any information about this child, please call the missing child hotline at: 1-800-ChildFind."

"He's back." Janice whispered to the empty room. "I knew he'd come back. But, we're going to catch him this time."

She dumped her unfinished cereal into the kitchen sink and picked up the phone. Child Find answered on the first ring.

"You have reached 1-800-ChildFind, this is Amea, do you have information regarding a missing child?"

Janice's mouth had gone so dry that she found it hard to speak, at first.

"Yes." She ran some water into a glass and gulped it down. "Yes. I have information regarding the abduction of the DeLapis girl."

"Okay. Can I have your name, please?"

"Yes. It is Janice Shuster. S-h-u-s-t-e-r."

"And where are you calling from, Ms. Shuster?"

"I am calling from Fredericksburg, Virginia."

"Okay. This phone call is being recorded. Please tell me what you know about this case."

"I believe this is the work of the 'Shortcut Stalker,' Jack Garrett. This is the way he always took the young girls. He would wait along popular shortcuts and grab his victims."

"Didn't those murders take place ten years ago?"

"Yes."

"What makes you think that he is back?"

Janice exhaled her exasperation.

"My best friend was taken by Jack Garrett ten years ago. I know his M.O. Besides, I just have this gut feeling. . ."

"But, you haven't seen this child and have no other knowledge of this case?"

"No, but."

Would you like to leave contact information, Ms. Shuster?"

"Yes."

Feeling as though she was being brushed off as a loony, Janice left her name and number for the operator and hung up the phone. Charlottesville. It was only an hour away. Could he be stupid enough to come back to Virginia and start taking children again? If so, she was going to make sure he didn't get away this time.

Her next call was to the Fredericksburg police precinct. "Could I speak to Officer Gentry, please?"

"I'm sorry, he has retired from the force. Could someone else be of assistance?"

"No. Thank you. It's nothing urgent."

Yes it is!

Janice hung up and stood for a long minute, staring at the phone. What was she going to do? How was she going to get anyone to believe her?

She dropped into a chair by the kitchen table and sipped her water, slowly. A plan of action was gradually coming together behind her closed eyes. There were things she could do, and she would do them. For Charity's sake.

12. THE "WORK" END OF IT

Separating one section from another always brought that first buck to mind, and how his father had looked on with pride as he had sawed away at the carcass. Jack missed his father sometimes. Though he tried not to, he still felt some responsibility for the old man's death. And Eddie...Poor Eddie.

True to his word, he had taken his little brother out for target practice every chance he got. Gradually, Eddie even got pretty good at using his rifle. So good, that they were both looking forward to their hunting trip that winter.

They had found the cabin much as they remembered it, and a spirit of camaraderie had enveloped the three of them that had seemed miraculous at the time. The last morning of his life, his father had made pancakes for breakfast. He'd even let Jack have his first cup of coffee. It had been strong and bitter; awful, really. But, Jack had finished every last drop and asked for a refill.

Right out of the box, Eddie bagged his first buck. It was a 10-pointer, and Dad had slapped Eddie's back and exclaimed, "That's the way, son! That's the way! Good shot! Best shot a man ever made!"

But, as John Emile Garrett, Sr. kneeled by the fresh kill, another shot rang out. Jack saw his Dad fall with a shocked expression on his face – his hand to his chest; blood running between his fingers. When Jack turned his head, he had seen the truth. Eddie had killed their father with one, well-placed, shot. *A shot to be proud of, really.*

Jack's reverie ended abruptly when he heard a car crunching down the gravel drive towards the barn. *Who the fuck?*

He wiped his hands on an old towel that hung on a hook behind him and removed his gore-encrusted apron. A quick backwards glance at his current "Project" and he was out the barn doors and into the bright mid-day sun. He was fiddling with the padlock when an old green Buick rolled to a stop behind him. He turned, slowly, and raised a hand to shield his eyes from the glare.

"Mr. Gormsley?"

"Yes?"

"Oh! I'm so glad to have finally caught you in! My name is Janice Schuster. I've left several messages."

"Miss Schuster!" Jack's heart stopped for a long minute. *Damnit!* He should have returned her calls. "Yes, of course. I'm so sorry to have been slow in responding. Just call me Earnest, please. No need to stand on formalities. I had every intention of contacting you earlier, but, these are difficult times for family farms." He waved his hand to encompass the cluster of outbuildings and pens of livestock.

"Yes. I'm sure they are." She smiled, engagingly.

Cute, but too old. He appraised her attributes with a practiced purity of intent. She was in her early twenties, long, blonde hair; unusually tall, but shapely; very nice.

"You were looking for a man? Correct? Somebody who might have owned this property at one time?"

"Yes." She sighed and handed him a flyer. He gave it a cursory inspection and felt his mouth twitch when he saw the artist's rendering of himself. The hair was graying, collar length, thick and wavy; startling blue eyes stared out behind wire-rimmed glasses, and all of this sitting atop a pair of fine, muscular shoulders. Somebody must have used an age progression program on his old driver's license photo. He wanted to giggle. Earnest Gormsley was completely bald, with dark brown eyes and a graying goatee. This pretty little piece of fluff posed no threat to Jack Garrett, or anyone else. His eyes glittered with amusement.

"His name is John Emile Garrett, Jr., but he goes by 'Jack.' Have you ever seen him around town, or do you know where he might have gone after he sold the place?"

"Hmm. Nice looking young man." He coughed. "You say he murdered somebody?"

"Yes sir. My dearest friend, Charity. She was only 15 at the time."

"Fifteen! Oh, no. So young." He handed the flyer back to her.

"There were five little girls taken, actually. All of them raped and murdered."

"Why that's just beyond wicked. Who could use a tender child in such a way?"

"Jack Garrett would, sir. In fact, he may be doing it again. Two young girls have gone missing in the last month under similar circumstances. That's why I need any information I can find. Do you remember anything about the man who sold you this land?"

"Nope. I'm sorry, young lady. I should have called; would have saved you the trip out here. I bought the farm from a realty company. Never met the previous owner. Never laid eyes on him."

"Would you remember the name of the Realtor, by any chance? Even the company would be a help."

"Oh, goodness no. You'll understand, maybe, when you've got a few more years on you, but people my age only save space for the important bits, like what we had for breakfast." He chuckled, then followed her gaze to his right boot. Blood.

"Oh. You'll have to pardon that. Been slaughtering a hog just this minute. Messy business, that."

"Ah. Yes. I guess it is." She handed the flyer back to him. "Please keep this. Show it to your neighbors, or anybody who might have known him. My number is on the bottom, you can call any time - night or day - with information."

"Are you conducting this search on your own, honey? What about the police? FBI?"

She looked down and scuffed some dirt with her tennis shoe. "No. I'm afraid they've run out of steam, Mr. Gormsley." At his hand raised in protest she said "Um; 'Earnest.' The case went cold years ago."

"But, not for you, eh?" He patted her warmly on the back -- ushering her towards the Buick.

"Never for me."

"Well, you are to be commended. Yes, you are! I wish there were more young people like yourself in this here world."

"Charity was somebody special." A breeze troubled her hair and she moved to hook the offending piece behind her ear. "Anyway, please call me if anybody remembers anything? I mean, anything at all."

"Will do. You have my word on it, little missy. Anything old Earnest here can do to help a damsel in distress."

She climbed into the driver's seat and flashed him a million-dollar smile. He was honestly taken-aback by it. What a charmer she was.

"Thank you. The tiniest clue could make all the difference, and I won't rest until that monster has paid for what he did to Charity."

"And, neither will I, Miss Schuster; neither will I." Jack eased the car door closed and lifted his hand to wave. He kept a fatherly smile in place until Janice Schuster was just a cloud of dust on the horizon. As her car disappeared, his visage morphed easily into one of grim resolve.

Now, back to work. This monster still had a "dear" that needed tending to. As Jack fumbled with the lock to the barn, he remembered getting the phone call. It had been such a shock.

He had dropped into the dilapidated blue recliner at the time that had always been his Dad's, and he had come closer to crying than he ever had or ever would. Eddie had been taken to a mental health facility shortly after the shooting. Three months later, an orderly had found him hanging by the rod in his closet. It had been too late to save him.

The world that had never wanted little Eddie in the first place, was rid of him before his fourteenth birthday. Wherever Eddie was, he hoped that his mother was there to protect him.

13. JANICE RULES

Satisfied with her day's work, Janice pulled into the Dairy Queen drive through for a Strawberry-CheeseQuake Blizzard®.   Still slender and fit ten years after the abduction of Charity, she rarely passed up an opportunity to reward herself for efforts above and beyond the call of duty. She had never considered herself an outgoing person, so handing flyers to strangers and canvassing communities for information about a serial murderer on the run was something she had to dig deep for. In such situations, it had always helped to channel her powerhouse cousin from Nashville. If Janice could mimic Andrea's confident walk and engaging mannerisms, then everything else usually fell into place.

She pulled into a shady spot and put all the windows down. It was a hot day, but every now and then, a breeze would cool the sweat that had beaded up on her face, neck and arms. The first spoonful of ice cream was pure heaven, as was every spoonful after that. Gradually, she began to cool down and relax.

There had been something odd about that farmer, Mr. Gormsley. She scraped the spoon around all of the edges of the cup to get the last remnants of melted ice cream that had gathered in the seams. He had been nice enough; certainly not threatening in any way. *But that blood on his boots and jeans.* She shuddered. There had been gobbets of flesh mixed in with it, and the smell coming off him had been just. . . *overpowering*. And, wasn't it odd the way he had smiled when he had looked at Jack Garret's face. Why would anybody smile under those circumstances? She felt as though he had been laughing at her, and it wasn't a nice laugh at all.

Janice crumpled the cup and put it, along with the sleek red spoon and plastic domed lid into the bag she had been using for trash since she had left home yesterday afternoon. Her fingers were sticky in spots, so she licked them, absentmindedly.

He might not have known which company had handled his sale, but there were land records she could research, with copies of settlement papers, too – no doubt – in the Hall of Records downtown. She was suddenly very curious about that transaction.

Immediately after the police found Mr. Garrett's wrecked truck abandoned about a block from Charity's house, they had issued search warrants for all Virginia properties held in his name. What they hadn't realized at the time was that Jack owned land in Maryland and Pennsylvania, as well. While those properties had eventually been ferreted out and searched for bodies, Jack had already somehow managed to sell a few of them and liquidate the assets.

The farm that Mr. Gormsley now owned had been searched like all of the others, but it had been clean. Not a trace of evidence had been found. The deed had been neatly transferred somehow, and Janice had just made up her mind to find out how. Her instincts were telling her that something was not right about Mr. Gormsley or his "Farm."

She leaned back in the seat and closed her eyes for a few minutes; allowing her mind to pick through the images she had carried away from her encounter with Mr. Gormsley. There were the boots, the blood, flesh. . . Janice sat bolt upright. Now, she knew what had bothered her all along. There had been hairs, long, blonde hairs stuck to the gore on his pants leg. Not the kinds of hair one often attributed to hogs. . .

Oh my God! She thought about his height, and the shape of his face. The eyes were wrong, though; brown. Jack's had been a startling blue. *Isn't that easy enough to change these days? Ever heard of contact lenses?*

Her heart was pounding as she struggled to catch her breath. Suddenly, she knew where to find Jack Garrett. Didn't she? Or, was her imagination just filling in the blanks? The local police would probably either ignore her outright, or bungle things badly and give Gormsley a chance to run. She had to reach Officer Gentry from the Fredericksburg Police department. He had been the first officer on the scene after Charity's disappearance. Even though he had recently retired, she knew that this case had taken on a special importance to him over the years, and he just might be willing to listen to what she had to say.

But, first Janice had to make a trip to the Hall of Records downtown. She would need as much information as she could get her hands on to make a believable case.

"Help me, Charity, wherever you are?" She started up the Buick and headed back towards town, knowing that Charity had moved on long ago and wasn't there to hear her plea.

14. OFFICER GENTRY

Janice walked into the police precinct with all of the confidence she could muster. She didn't know why, but policemen had always made her nervous. Even though she knew she hadn't done anything wrong, she always felt guilty when they were around.

Everything in the foyer had been updated since the last time she had been there. Large plants, modern furniture, and flashy artwork blended blues and whites with occasional splashes of orange to make it look more inviting. The officer at the front desk looked just as intimidating as he always had, though. She gulped and approached him, hoping that she didn't look like a criminal.

She clutched a large envelope full of the copies she had made at the Hall of Records. She read the nameplate that was prominently displayed on the counter. *Officer Timothy Mann*. Suddenly, all of her "evidence" seemed a bit lame.

"How can I help you, today." The officer asked, looking up from some paperwork.

"Hi. My name is Janice Schuster, and I need to speak to Officer Gentry about a possible lead in one of his cold cases?"

"Ah. Well, I'd be happy to help you with that, but Officer Gentry retired last December. Could anyone else help you? Maybe if you tell me about the case, I could point you in the right direction?"

"Yes. I know he has retired, but do you know how I could reach him? It was Officer Gentry that I really needed to talk to. This is pretty important."

"Sorry, miss. . ." He struggled to remember her name.

"Schuster."

"Yes. Sorry, miss Schuster, but I am not allowed to give out personal information on our officers. Perhaps you could leave a name and phone number with me and I could ask him to contact you, instead?"

She glowed. "Yes! Thank you, very much! That would be perfect."

"What should I tell him this is about?"

"Oh, he'll know. "

"Okay. Write everything down right here, and I'll pass your message on to him, directly."

Janice scribbled her name, phone, and the note, "I think I know where to find him. Need your help!"

"Thank you so much. Please try to call him right away? This is urgent."

He took the note from her and looked concerned. "Are you in any kind of trouble? We have officers here who would be happy to help you with whatever this is."

"No. Not at all. I really need to talk with Officer Gentry. He knows me and will listen. If he wants me to talk to someone here, I'll come back."

Still clutching her envelope, Janice walked out of the foyer and into the muggy Virginia sunshine. She had left her windows down, but could see waves of heat coming of the hood of her car, and braced herself for the searing hot leather seat and her stifling drive home. She reached into her pocket and pulled out her cell phone, set her ringer to full volume, and hoped for the best.

She knew that sharing this information with Gentry was the best option. He wanted Jack Garrett as much, or more, as she did. If she was right, the whole nightmare could be laid to rest.

Janice thought about calling Billy – Charity's brother – but decided against it. If she was wrong, then getting his hopes up too soon would be devastating. She thought about telling her mother, but ruled that out, as well. No. She would have to carry this knowledge alone for the time being.

Tucking the phone back into her pocket, she slid into the driver's seat, started up the old car, and headed for home.

15. JUST ME AND THE MRS.

The Gormsley's were known throughout the county as a quiet, happily-married, couple. They were active voices in the farming community, and could always be counted on to contribute to the local Fire Hall or the annual Policemen's Ball. Never missed a Sunday meeting at the Southern Baptist Church.

They were regulars at Barry's Diner at the corner of Fifth and Main. A quiet couple. The types that like to stay private and keep to themselves. The only people seen coming and going from their property were the farmhands that changed as often as the seasons. Rumor had it that Mr. Gormsley was "right particular" about his hogs, and could be a difficult person to work for.

Neither one of them was much to look at. He was tall and gangly, balding and scruffy. She was short and snub-nosed; you could say she more closely resembled his hogs than a woman, and you would be right. But, most found them easy enough to get along with.

Earnest had worked hard to create himself anew, and he never worried about being mistaken for a serial murderer named "Jack Garrett." His wife, Greta, had been plucked from the personals like an ear of corn from a stalk. She was as uninterested in him and he was in her, but was happy to have a husband with a successful farm to brag about, and to be saved from the humiliation of being called an old maid. She served his purposes well, and was a damn good cook into the bargain!

They had been married for only four years, but he made sure that he was seen about town with her on his arm, and that he treated her with great kindness in every regard. Nobody would look to a happily married, skinny hog farmer to find a depraved pedophile and ruthless killer of young girls.

For the first three years, he had been careful. It hadn't been easy to put off his insatiable desires, but he had known that there was no choice in the matter. The law was hot on his heels, and was not about to let up. But, now, years later, safely "reborn" to these new surroundings, it was time to venture out in search of prey.

It had been easy to pick his target from the church congregation. Sitting there in his usual balcony pew, he had been afforded a perfect view of all the innocent youth to be had. Their hair was curled and tied up in pretty ribbons; they were dressed in frilly pastels and lace, with those sweet little tights and patent leather shoes that he so adored.

Right about that time, Earnest had started purchasing cars. The fixer-uppers that could be parked around the back of the property or set up on cinderblocks for the weeds to grow up around. They didn't have license plates. They weren't registered or insured. Some of them ran like tops, and some of them didn't run at all. Who could say? There were so many of them.

Greta complained about this new hobby to anyone who would listen. Saying that her husband was "A very important man, and should not be having those 'heaps of trashes' on their farm." And also that "We have good cars, each of us. Better than anybody. Why we need those cars of peasants would drive?"

He knew that he wouldn't be the first Virginia farmer to clutter up the edges of his land with projects he might never get to. It made a brilliant cover for him, and gave him a wonderful source of "get-away" transportation that could be easily hidden from view in an instant.

His first target had been nine or ten years old. She was an angelic blonde child with long, honey-blonde hair who sang the hymns so sweetly it had been impossible to think about anything else for weeks.

When it was announced from the pulpit that volunteers were needed build a new playground at the elementary school, Earnest raised his hand. Greta had not been pleased, and he'd felt her elbow in his ribs.

"You are an old man. Let the parents do that work. You have enough work to be doing." She had hissed.

But, Earnest would not be dissuaded. After all, he loved children. Loved them more than just about anybody.

16.   HARD TO LET GO

It was 9:30 a.m. on a Tuesday morning. Under the rumpled sheets of their old-fashioned queen-sized bed, Mike and Virginia Gentry were still asleep. That happened more and more, these days. Since he retired, there was no reason to get up early. The kids had left home years ago, and Bob Evans served breakfast all day.

When the phone rang on Ginny's nightstand, they had both looked at it as though it were a purple Yeti. When was the last time that had rung? Christmas? They stared it into silence.

"What was that all about?" Mike grumbled. Check the caller ID and see who that was."

"Why? It was probably some cruise line or time share scam." She rolled to face him. "Let's snooze for a while, honey. It's supposed to be a rainy day. C'mon, let me cuddle up a bit."

He relaxed, pulled her close and shut his eyes. But, eventually, the cop in him won out. Mike gently disentangled his limbs from hers and slipped out of bed. As was more often than not the case these days, his first stop was the bathroom.

Before he could even get over to the antiquated Caller ID box, Mike's cell phone had begun to ring. He walked in the general direction of the sound.

"Goddamnit-all, where is it?" He stubbed his big toe on the sharp-cornered footboard and took off jumping around in circles with the injured foot in his hands. "VIRGINIA!"

She sat up and took in the scene with lazy amusement. "What did you do to yourself now, old man?"

The phone stopped ringing.

"Where is my cell phone?"

"Mike. How am I supposed to know what you did with your cell phone?"

"I don't know what's going on, my dear sweet love, but somebody seems dead set on getting through our defenses." They both chuckled as he hopped over to sit on the bed.

"Why don't you see if anybody left a message?"

Mike eyed his wife with chagrin. "Do you know how to get messages off this phone since we got that high-speed internet thing?"

"Well. No. I used to. Isn't there a number that you dial and then you press some more numbers?"

"Right."

"Okay. I'm up now. Let's find your cell phone. It's got to be around here, somewhere."

"You look in here, and I'll check the kitchen table."

"I'll do that, but only if you start the coffee while you're in there."

He kissed her on the nose. "You've got a deal."

She found it in the hamper; tucked into the pocket of his favorite khakis. "Got it!" she called at the top of her voice.

Mike walked through the door with a steaming mug of coffee and traded it for the phone.

"Aha! Did I ever tell you that you would have made an excellent detective?"

Virginia waved his flattery away and focused on the coffee. It was steaming hot and strong and black, just the way she liked it.

"It's the office. Tim wants me to call him back right away. That's odd. What could they possibly want with me?"

"Maybe you left something behind?"

"Nope. Never kept any personal stuff around.

"Well. What are you waiting for?"

He shrugged and pushed four – (the office auto-dial).

"Fredericksburg Police, Officer Mann."

"Tim? It's Mike. What's going on over there? You've got the Mrs. and me awful curious this morning."

"Hey, Mike! How are things going? I'm sorry to bother you. Did I call too early? Fact is, I was supposed to call you yesterday, and forgot all about it."

"Naw. We were awake. No problem. So? What's this about?"

"Well, yesterday afternoon a gorgeous young blonde walked in looking for you." Mike loved the familiar leer in Tim's voice.

"Okay. You've got my attention."

"She left you a note. Here, I'll read it

"I think I know where to find him. Need your help!"

"That's the whole message?"

"Well, she did leave a phone number and a first name, 'Janice?' Does that ring any bells?'"

The silence stretched out between them.

"Mike? You still there?"

Could Janice have located Jack Garrett? How could she have done what the entire Fredericksburg police force and the FBI had been unable to do over the last ten years?

"Mike."

"Um." He cleared his throat. "Yeah. I'm still here. Sorry; was distracted for a minute. You know how us old men get."

"Ha. You haven't been out of the game long enough to lose your edge, so don't even try that one on."

"Let me get that number from you. Just a minute."

"Virginia? Could you get me a pen and something to write on, please?" Mike whispered, placing his hand over the receiver.

Wordlessly, Virginia opened the bedside table drawer under the obsolete phone and found the pad of paper and pen that had always been kept on hand in those bygone days when a land line had still been considered a necessity.

Mike accepted the items from her and nodded his thanks.

"Okay. Fire away."

"The number is (555) 325-5525."

Mike repeated the number and thanked Officer Mann.

"You stay safe, will you?"

"Will do. You do the same.

Virginia watched her husband of 50 years as he stared, wonderingly, at the yellow slip of paper in his hands.

"So? Are you going to tell me what is going on?"

"Janice Schuster stopped by the precinct and left me a message. She seems to think. . ."

"Janice? Janice. Why does that sound familiar?

"She thinks she knows where Jack Garrett – the Shortcut Stalker – is hiding out."

There was a sharp intake of breath, and Virginia moved to drape an arm around his shoulders. "That would be wonderful, wouldn't it? Do you think she really found him? Sounds a bit too good to be true."

"That's what I'm thinking, too. She never gave up. Well, neither did I. Retiring without putting that sick bastard away was one of the hardest things I've ever had to do."

"So? Aren't you going to call her? What are you standing around for?"

"I guess I should. Tim said she left the message yesterday and he forgot all about it until this morning. I bet she's somewhere staring at the phone."

Virginia sat down on the edge of the bed, crossed the fingers on both hands and held them up to show support.

Mike dialed the number and waited for the call to connect. After only two rings, Janice was on the other end.

"Officer Gentry?"

"That's me. I just got your message, Janice. Do you really think. . . Is it about Jack?"

Her voice was breathless; as though she had just run up a flight of stairs.

"Yes. I think I've found him. You won't believe this, but he's working a hog farm not two hours out of town."

"A hog farm?"

"I know. Look, I've got some stuff I'd like to show you. Can we meet somewhere?"

"Sure. Why don't you come over here? My wife and I will fix you a nice lunch, and . . ."

"Okay. Give me an address and I'll head over right now."

Officer Gentry patiently gave her his street name and number.

"What makes you think it's Jack? What would he be doing on a hog farm?"

"I know it sounds crazy." She sounded discouraged. "That's why I refused to talk to anybody else about it. All I ask is that you take a look at what I've found and see if you agree."

"Do you have a photo of the guy?"

"No. Nothing that good. But, I've been face-to-face with him, and I just *know*."

17. NO HAM, PLEASE

Officer Gentry lived on the other side of town. Janice would never make the trip with the bright "E" that was blinking hungrily from her dashboard.

"Mom?"

"No."

"What? How can you say 'no' when you haven't heard the question?"

"No. You want gas money, and I told you that the only way you're going to get gas money is to go out and get a job like everybody else."

"What I'm doing is important."

"What? Chasing down a murderer? I know you miss Charity, and I try to understand this crazy mission you have assigned yourself; but, I don't have to finance it."

"I found something really important to the case, though. I'm going over to Officer Gentry's house to tell him about it."

"Tell me that you're not bothering that man with one of your far-fetched theories? He has heard them all, by now, I'm sure; and didn't I hear that he had retired from the force?"

"Mom."

"No."

Janice let out a heavy sigh before trying again.

"What if I promise to cook dinner for the rest of the week?"

"And, do the dishes?"

"And do the dishes." She promised with gravity.

She could see her mother wavering, and took advantage of the opportunity.

"All I need is $15! Please? I just need to get there and get back. He is expecting me, Mom. His wife is making us lunch!"

The purse came out and the wallet was opened just far enough to slip out a $20. Janice took the bill before her mother could have a change of heart.

"Thanks, Mom!" She planted the obligatory kiss on her mother's cheek. "You're a lifesaver."

With gas in the tank, Janice hit the road. She had been so deep in thought that she almost drove right past the Gentry home and had to stand on the brakes to make the left into their driveway.

The house was modest. Janice had expected to see something more elaborate. Still, the landscaping was amazing: Azaleas of three different colors surrounded by gentle beds of Phlox in blue and white. She had been happy to see the central air compressor, as well, and could hardly wait to get out of her suffocating Buick and into the cool shadows she was imagining awaited her inside.

Just as she was reaching for the doorbell, the front door came open and there was Mrs. Gentry; slender and elegant in a brightly-flowered skirt and a sleeveless white top.

"So. You're this Janice I've heard so much about!" She said gaily

"That would be me." Janice turned her smile on full force; and it didn't take any effort at all.

"He hasn't stopped fidgeting since he got your message this morning. Come on into the kitchen and we'll talk over some sandwiches and lemonade."

"Janice!"

Another full-on smile, and then she was hugging Officer Gentry like an old friend. "Hello. How have you been, Officer Gentry? I've thought about you so many times."

"Do you believe it has been. . . "

"Ten years. . . I know. I'm hoping that we can end it all for good this time."

"I'm for that! Here, sit down and let's see what you've got in that packet of yours."

"Janice held on tight to the envelope as she sat at the table opposite Officer Gentry."

"I was able to find some of what I was looking for in the way of evidence, but, I'll admit my case is pretty slim. This is something you are just going to have to take my word on."

Mike looked deeply into her eyes, and she didn't flinch away or look to the right or left. I know how much this means to you. Don't you think it's possible that you are reaching into the realm of positive thinking?"

"No. I don't think so. Let me tell you why."

They had turkey sandwiches on toasted rolls that were wonderful. Between bites of sandwich and sips of lemonade, Janice shared her experience with Earnest Gormsley. Not leaving anything out, she opened up the packet she had brought and put the meager evidence out – sheet by sheet. The land records had shown deed to the farm as having been transferred to Mr. Gormsley for only $500. So, why would Earnest say that he had purchased it from a real estate company? Officer Gentry's eyebrows rose as he examined the documents.

The last sheet had been her own composite sketch of the hog farmer. No artist, she had been hesitant to attempt it, but felt that a comparison between the two visages might strengthen her assertion.

As Janice finished talking, she watched Officer Gentry for signs of disbelief and was relieved to see there weren't any.

"So, you are sure that you saw long hairs in the gore that was stuck to his pants?

"Yes sir. I know it sounds crazy." She sounded discouraged. "He was just so smug and condescending. It was as though he was saying 'I'm Jack Garrett' what are you going to do about it."

"Okay. Let's say you're right and he is Jack Garrett in disguise. What would you like me to do now?"

She moved a lock of hair behind her ear and gulped. This was going to be the hard part.

"I want you to compare his DNA with what you gathered from Jack's truck."

"I don't have access to that kind of testing, any more, but let's say I could cash in some old favors. . . Do you have any of Earnest Gormsley's DNA?"

"No." She murmured. "But, I know where I can get some."

Their eyes met and locked. "Do you think you can get it without becoming victim number 6?"

"Number 8, if I'm right; and, yes."

"Eight?"

"Two girls have been reported missing within 60 miles of his farm. They disappeared under similar circumstances, and their bodies have never been found."

"When?"

"Within the last six months. The last one, only a few days before I met him outside his locked shed."

Mike sat quietly, then. Clearly weighing everything he had just heard. "Have the police made any connections to our case?"

"No. Well, actually. . . I don't know."

"You are making some pretty wild leaps here, young lady, but I'm willing to trust your instincts."

Her smile would have lit up a moonless night on Mars.

"So? Do we have a deal? Will you help me?"

18. BILLY FISCHE

An athletically built, 17-year-old heartthrob; Billy Fische stood in front of his closet in a football jersey and a pair of boxers. He shoved each hangar aside with a grim expression on his face. Two pairs of jeans had already been pushed aside -- they weren't the right ones.

"MOM!" He put his hands on his hips and checked his alarm clock. *Crap.*

"MOM! Where are my dark jeans?" Getting no reply, he marched over to his door and leaned into the hallway.

"MOM!"

His mother reached the top of the stairs and turned towards him. "What in God's name are you hollering about? And, why aren't you dressed?" It was her turn to scan the clock. "You are going to be late for school – again."

"I know it. I'm sorry. I can't find my dark jeans. You know the ones I'm talking about, right? The ones --"

"That you wear every single day? Those dark jeans?" She grinned.

"Yeah. C'mon, Mom, I'm in a hurry."

"Well, I am not an expert on such things, but, if it were me, I'd be tempted to dig through that pile of clothes on the floor."

Billy tossed the items aside - one at a time - until he hit gold. "Yep! Here they are! Thanks, Mom."

He plopped onto the side of his bed and jammed both legs into the jeans. Running too late to start hunting clean socks, he hesitated only slightly before pulling on the ones he'd worn yesterday and sliding on his shoes. Laces still untied, Billy took the stairs two at a time and flew through the front door – slamming it behind him.

Two seconds later, the door flew open again, and Billy ran inside and scooped up his forgotten book bag before making his second exit of the morning.

The bus stop was deserted. He'd missed it and would have to hoof it to school. Though it wasn't even 7:00 a.m., the heat was substantial enough to thicken the air and make each step a challenge.

Crap.

When he reached the shortcut through Harlan's Woods, Billy slowed a bit. He thought about Charity. His mouth was dry and his freshly-showered body was already slick with sweat. He pulled the jersey loose from his stomach and waved it a bit to let in some air.

Charity.

He picked his way down the trail to where the umbrella had been found that night. He thought a brief "I miss you, Sis," and picked up speed.

He would never forget the visits Charity paid him after her abduction and murder. It wasn't something he talked about, but nobody had ever been able to convince him that he had been having some kind of vivid dream. There was part of him that always hoped she would come back, but he knew that she had gone on to wherever spirits are supposed to go, and he was glad she was at peace.

Billy had a pretty good idea who was behind the accident that had put a stop to Jack Garrett's truck that day. He smiled, wishing that he knew how she'd pulled it off. Charity had been pretty awesome.

He was angry that the police and the FBI had not been able to arrest his sister's murderer even after finding his truck wrecked at the end of their street. They had everything they needed to get that guy! His drivers' license, address, photo, fingerprints. . . But, here it was, ten years since his sister's death, and there had been no arrest made in her case.

The murders and abductions in Fredericksburg had stopped. At least, Charity had been able to do that much. She had put Jack Garrett on the run. A girl! And a dead girl at that!

Billy had seen some strange things since Charity's first visit; an injured woman standing in the chapel who disappeared when he went to offer assistance; a small child on the swings at the park that faded away to nothing – leaving the swing in motion with no occupant. Talking about these things had been a huge mistake. People didn't believe him – even looked at him with a worried expression.

He was pretty sure that he had some kind of psychic 'gift.' Maybe, that was why he had been able to see and hear Charity so clearly when others had not? Thankfully, the sights and sounds of the departed had never frightened him. Billy was able to concentrate most of his attention on the ups and downs of being 17.

At the first sight of the kids piling out of the buses and pushing their way into the high school, he poured on an extra burst of speed. His backpack felt as though it had gained twenty pounds since he left home.

The first bell rang as he joined the press of adolescent humanity that was pouring into the building and flowing noisily through the halls to class.

19. DNA

Getting a DNA sample from the mysterious Mr. Gormsley should have been a simple matter. After all, he was probably feeling perfectly safe in his assumed identity. Janice thought about waiting until the couple left for church on Sunday and driving down the long, packed-dirt drive to the farm. The horrible shed would be locked, of course. Perhaps she would be able to rummage through the trash or . . .

And what if you get caught? Janice cut the top of a foil packet marked "Cheese" and dumped yellow powder into a saucepan containing hot macaroni noodles and melted butter. She stirred the mess together with a wooden spoon.

There has to be a better way. A safer way.

The oven timer went off, making her jump. The chicken breasts were done. Taking the mac-and-cheese off the stove and replacing its lid, she then thrust her hand into a bright blue oven mitt and pulled out the broiling pan. Janice sliced her piece of chicken through the center to make sure they were done. The meat was white, juicy and firm. Perfect.

What about the Diner? Did the Gormsleys eat there? If so, when?

As a last step, Janice positioned a can of green beans under the electric can opener and pushed the "start" lever. The noise was jarring. Not for the first time, she wondered what had been wrong with the old-fashioned, quiet one that you cranked around the edges until the lid came free. The beans and most of the water they had been packed in were poured into a small casserole dish and placed in the microwave for two minutes on "high."

"Dinner's ready!" She called into the adjoining family room where her mother was kicking back and watching some TV.

Setting the table with the barest of necessities, Janice arranged the food on each plate. She was in the process of putting ice into the glasses when her mother pulled her chair up to the table.

"Hmm. Well, it isn't exactly gourmet, but I suppose it will do."

"Oh, c'mon, Mom. It's hot out and I've been doing laundry all day."

Her mother laughed, gleefully. "Yes. I know."

Janice gave each of them a tall, cold glass of iced tea before sinking into a chair. "You can laugh all you want to. I'm exhausted."

"Really? I can't imagine?"

Catching her sarcasm, Janice smiled. "Okay. I get it. I should help more often."

"I appreciate the help more than you know." She said, sipping her tea. "Definitely worth the gas money I'm forking out for that dinosaur of yours."

"Hey. Lay off my car! It gets me where I'm going and starts when I turn the key – what more could you want?"

"A smaller gas tank, for starters."

"Yeah. Well, I can't argue with you, there."

The first forkful of mac-and-cheese was heavenly. Sure, it was a cheap box mix, but it tasted like childhood and summer and. . .

"Where are you going that you need all of that gasoline? I hope you are job hunting, but I guess that would be too much to ask."

"Mom. I've tried. I've got applications out all over town."

"Well, if you're not job hunting. . ." Her mother's pause was full of meaning. Janice heaved a sigh, and put her head in her hands.

"I'm searching down leads."

"Come again?"

"Leads. I'm looking for Jack Garrett."

"Janice. When are you going to let that go? There hasn't been a murder here since that man ran out of town with his pants on fire."

"Not here, but. . ."

"What? What are you going on about?"

"There have been two more victims in the last six months. I think – no – I'm sure it's him."

"Where? Two? What makes you think . . ."

"Yes. Two girls over in Charlottesville. One was last seen before cutting through the park on her way home from a convenience store, the other was knocked off her bike on the trail next to the power station."

There was a long silence between them. Their eyes met.

"Have you told the police about your theory?"

"Yes. Sort-of..."

"Sort of?"

"I went to see Officer Gentry. He was the only person I could trust to understand. He was there."

"And, what did Officer Gentry have to say?"

"He is going to cash in some favors with the department and see what he can find out."

"Hmm?"

"He retired last December."

"Janice. Really. You shouldn't have bothered him with such a thing. He is probably trying to find some peace in his later years; to forget about all of those little girls and what they found on Garrett's property." She shuddered, remembering the reports of disinterred barrels filled with little body parts and lime.

"Mom. I can't let this happen again. Somebody needs to stop him now. We were there. We know what he does and how he does it. This is him. I just know it in my bones."

Janice stopped talking. If her mother ever found out about her suspicions and her plans to trap a certain hog farmer in Charlottesville, she would probably find herself tethered to a tree like a naughty dog.

"Well, now that you've alerted Mr. Gentry to the possibility, I'm sure he'll follow through using the appropriate channels. You've done your civic duty, and, I must say, I'm proud of you. Charity would be, too."

Janice took a savory bite of chicken breast; waiting for the other shoe to fall.

"BUT, a young woman your age who doesn't have a summer job should be ashamed of herself. Get out there and find something. Anything. Your classes won't pay for themselves, you know, and time's a'wasting!"

With a forkful of green beans halfway to her mouth, Janice had an idea. Hadn't she seen a "Help Wanted" sign in the window of the diner?

Why not?

Excited now, she cleaned her plate and downed her iced tea. *Talk about killing two flies with one swatter!*

20. THE EAGER VOLUNTEER

At 11:00 a.m. that Saturday, it was already gearing up to be a scorcher. Earnest had shown up early with his tools and an ice chest full of sodas and bottled water for all of the volunteers. *(He was just a giving kind of guy).*

The elementary school's playground had a deserted air about it. You could look around and convince yourself that the adjacent school had been abandoned years earlier. Earnest shook his head. This was going to take more than a few coats of paint.

As other volunteers began to arrive, the futile nature of their task became the topic of discussion. The legs to the swing set were dented and the whole thing sat at an odd angle. Rust had eaten away at the slide to the point that some of the rungs of the ladder to the top were clearly a cause for concern.

Mrs. O'Connor, the school's new Vice Principal, joined them with a hopeful and enthusiastic demeanor; welcoming all of the volunteers and thanking them for re-building the beleaguered playground.

"Okay, Guys! Where do we start?" She bubbled over like a pot left to boil unattended.

There was a brief shuffling of feet and a few coughs from the assembled volunteers. All probably wondering how to state the obvious – this stuff was only good for the loose change they might get from the scrap yard.

Earnest Gormsley stepped up. "Ma'am. I hate to be the bearer of bad news, but the equipment is beyond any help that we could give it. The best we can do today is to haul it away before a child gets seriously injured."

Her face fell. She looked from one man to the next for validation, and then shrugged in defeat. "Well, I guess that's what we need to do, then. I don't know how we will ever be able to replace it, but . . ."

There was more shifting and shuffling as men gathered their saws and shovels. Gloves were pulled on and the work began. To her credit, Mrs. O'Connor worked as hard as any of the volunteers. The derelict play equipment was disassembled and carried off, piece by piece, until there was nothing left but dirt and weeds.

As the sun set, the exhausted volunteers packed up their tools and bid good night to one another. Their faces were smudged with dirt, rust and debris. Their hands were blistered, and more than one had a new cut or bruise to show for his efforts.

Every last one of them had envisioned leaving a freshly-painted and fully-repaired playground behind that day, but they had to find gratification in the joyless space they had been forced to conceive, instead.

With heavy hearts, they all drove off, leaving Mrs. O'Connor standing resolutely in the middle of the empty yard; her hands on her hips and fund-raising on her mind.

21. BARRY'S NEW DISHWASHER

It took all of 20 minutes for Janice to become the new dishwasher at Barry's Diner in Charlottesville. The pay was pretty lousy, but better than what she had been making so far that summer – and there were certain fringe benefits that came along with the position.

All she had to do now was wait for the Gormsley's to show up for breakfast, lunch or dinner. When the dishes came back to her, she could bag up his utensils, plate and drinking glass and turn them over to Officer Gentry for analysis. Even one fingerprint would suffice, as plenty of good prints were taken when his truck was confiscated ten years ago.

As Janice attacked her first pile of greasy dishes, she thought about the work that awaited her once she got home. It took a lot of household chores to earn the kind of money she would need to get out here four days a week. When the topic of shifts had come up, she had been quick to take the, (decidedly less-popular), Friday-to-Monday stint, as those were the days that the Gormsleys were most likely to appear.

Barry's was a popular meeting place for the locals, and Janice was now in a position to hear all of the juiciest bits of gossip. The Chef's name was "Mack Hogey," and his "Hogey's Hoagies" were a specialty of the house.

Mack was a no-nonsense guy. He was in his late 60's and had been serving up tasty entrees at Barry's for at least 20 of those. Though slow to warm up, he soon fell prey to Janice's winning ways, and was a veritable fountain of information on every living soul within 30 miles.

He knew about Earnest and Greta Gormsley, alright. According to Mack, they were as compatible as a hawk and a rabbit.

"That Earnest doesn't fool me for a minute. I don't know why he married that woman, but it wasn't for love nor money. I'm fairly certain that he's never heard a word that came out of her mouth – and, God knows, there were plenty of those."

"Old Earnest will sit there with his plate full of chicken livers and mashed potatoes and just stare off into space while she clucks and carries on. Now, don't get me wrong, he don't deny the old girl nothing. She may be the wealthiest woman in town – as a matter of fact -- and she doesn't make a secret of it, neither."

"Oh, one of those." Janice intoned.

"Yep. She's a braggart and a boaster the likes of which this town has never seen before. Why, if she were to put one more stone around her neck, I'd be tempted to drown her."

"Do hog farmers really bring home that kind of money?"

"Dunno about most of them. That Earnest Gormsley can sure rake in the dough. Far as I know, everybody buys their meat from his farm. He don't pay his farm hands enough to make ends meet. They come and go from that property like migrating birds; and the ones that's come in here didn't have a nice word to say about neither one of them."

"Word around town is that he inherited some tracts of land and made a pretty penny selling them off to some folks that meant to build condos."

"And, the farm's got to turn a profit. Everybody gets their meat from his farm. We get a regular delivery here at Barry's. Have for near unto ten years."

That timeframe rang a bell for Janice.

"What was it before it was a hog farm?"

Mack scratched his head and thought about it for a bit.

"Well, I could be wrong, but I think it was willed to this young feller that killed himself. Wasn't used for nothin' but weeds and wild things. Seems like his name was 'Freddy,' or 'Eddie,' something along those lines."

"Are you sure? I heard that land belonged to Jack Garrett at one time. You know, the "Shortcut Stalker."

"Garrett! There you go! Mebbe. It was his brother's land until he up and killed himself. Eddie Garrett. How could I have forgotten? Could just be that Jack was next in line for it. Now, that's a story. It would take me the better part of a week to tell it."

She flashed her award-winning smile. "Well, I have it on good authority that I'm going to be right here washing dishes through August."

He was happy to respond in kind. "That you will, Miss Schuster. That you will."

22. OUR HERO AND BENEFACTOR

Mrs. O'Connor was not expecting to have a crowd control problem so early in the morning. When she pulled up, instead of the wiggly lines of children waiting expectantly for the doors to open, the elementary school's receiving area was deserted. Getting out of her car, the sound of excited voices was easy to follow.

What is going on?

She followed the cacophony around to the back and couldn't believe what she was seeing. The playground. It was. . . beautiful! But, where had it all come from? She leaned against an ancient maple tree and stared in disbelief.

It looked to her as though somebody had purchased and installed every piece of play equipment ever manufactured. Bright horses, elephants and zebras were positioned atop thick springs for riding; a giant blue spider with a red nose and matching feet rolled it's comic eyes as children climbed over, around and through its eight sprawled appendages. The slide offered a spiral descent and a thick foam mat to land on.

This must have cost somebody a fortune.

The kids were swarming over everything like ants. Mrs. O'Connor and several other faculty members who had begun to wander into the melee were strangely okay with it. After all, how many miracles does one come across in a lifetime?

When Mr. and Mrs. Gormsley showed up – smiling copiously – the Vice Principal rushed to greet them.

"Did you do this?"

"Well. . . " He tried on a humility that didn't come naturally.

"Of course, we did!" Greta stood up to her full height with an off-putting arrogance. "Who else could have afforded to give such a gift but my Earnest?"

"You did! You are an angel! How did you manage to get it all done so quickly?"

"Let's just say I have many friends and associates who were willing to participate in such a project."

"It is a miracle. Truly." Mrs. O'Connor grabbed Earnest's hand in both of hers and then, overcome with emotion, she released that hand and wrapped him up in an enthusiastic embrace.

The Gormsleys had quite a reputation for being strange ducks, but, it didn't take long for news of this generous act to get around town. Grateful parents, grandparents, church parishioners, and local businessmen went out of their way to honor Earnest at every opportunity. (Greta, not so much. . .)

A special assembly was called so that the children could honor him with songs, banners and artwork. After the presentation, applause and laughter had filled the little auditorium. Earnest had smiled humbly from the podium – even shed a few tears. . .

Under that mask of humility and quiet emotion, Jack Garrett reveled in the opportunities this action would afford him. For, now he posed as a trusted member of society; a benefactor, a hero of sorts. Who would accuse such a pillar of society of committing crimes against innocent children?

As the presentation came to a close, several little girls ran up to hug Earnest's legs and giggle out their gratitude. Sweet little things, they were. Young, yet. But very, very sweet.

23. FREE FOOD FOR LIFE

When Janice arrived for work on Friday, Mack was brimming over with the news. She listened with disbelief as he praised Earnest Gormsley to the skies and told her how Barry had refused to take money when they showed up for dinner the night before – going so far as to say that "From now on, the Gormsleys eat free at Barry's Diner."

"They were here last night?" Janice deflated. She'd missed an opportunity to catch him.

"Yep! Guess you missed it. There was quite a hullaballoo. Just about everybody's got a kid, a grandkid, niece or nephew over at that school. You should see it, Janice. Really. He turned that place into Disneyland overnight."

"Isn't that just great." She plunged her hands into the dishwater and grabbed a glass.

"Whassa' matter? Don't you think that was a pretty neat thing he did?"

"Oh. Sure. I'm sorry, Mack. There's just something about him that doesn't ring true."

"Aw. He's okay. I was sour on him, too. He's not exactly your normal, everyday small-town guy. . ."

Not wanting to tip her hand, Janice switched tracks.

"Yeah. I guess you're right. That was a pretty great thing he did for the kids. Not sure why I took such an instant dislike to the guy."

"Oh, don't feel bad about that. Just about everybody did. He is pretty weird. You know, how he smiles at the wrong times and stares holes through you to where you can't think what you were saying in the first place. . . "

"That's really something about Barry. He strikes me as somebody who is fairly protective of his pocket change." She smiled wryly.

Mack laughed heartily and flipped some bacon. "Anybody ever tell you that you're a damn good judge of character?"

He poured scrambled eggs onto the grill and the air filled with the sizzle-pop-steam of them being scraped back and forth through the bacon grease with Mack's customary speed and precision.

"Do they come here often? The Gormsleys?"

"Pretty much every Sunday morning before Church."

Janice felt some tension flow out of her. Sunday. She would get the evidence she needed to put Earnest (or *Jack*) where he belonged. It worried her that he had been setting himself up as a kind of rural "Santa Claus" to the parents and children of Charlottesville. Gaining the trust of so many people would make it that much easier for him to isolate and prey on his victims. For Janice, Sunday couldn't come soon enough.

She finished out her 12-hour shift at 8:00 p.m. and prepared herself for the long trip home. It hadn't made sense to take a minimum-wage job with that kind of a commute. The cost of gas would effectively cancel out any money she earned. Thankfully, Janice's mother had been so pleased about her finding work and paying for her own gas that she had let the household chores slide.

Exhausted, Janice slipped into a hot tub as soon as she was able to wriggle out of her dirty uniform. Even though she didn't cook at Barry's, the constant smoking of the grill had covered her in a film of fragrant lard that played havoc with her complexion and left her feeling and smelling like a life-sized "Hogey's Hoagie."

She worked up a creamy lather of soap in her palms and massaged it gently into her face. It felt so good to splash the hot water over her tired eyes, and to feel Barry's Diner sliding away with the bubbles.

Tonight she would sleep – knowing that it would all be over soon. Jack Garrett was only a fork or a drinking glass away from being unmasked and imprisoned. It had all seemed so simple to her.

What could possibly go wrong?

24. A FOX IN THE HENHOUSE

Brown-eyed and bald-headed, Earnest Gormsley sat alone in his private workshop. In his lap was a crudely carved wooden box that he had made a lifetime ago in junior high school.

The simple hinge and latch had been secured with a small padlock to which only he held a key.

Greta had asked about it once. He shrugged the question off with a stupid grin. "Just mementos from my misspent youth, my dear."

Thankfully, for Greta, she had been more interested in getting some spending cash for a shopping excursion at the time. Being too inquisitive about Earnest (Jack Garrett) Gormsley's past was a very dangerous thing – whether she knew it or not.

Now, alone and locked safely within his fortified refuge, he reverently inserted the key and turned it with a "click."

This was his treasure. It was his happiness and held his lifetime achievements. It was his passion.

Secreted away in the trunk of a hollow tree in the graveyard where his Mother, Father and dear, deranged brother had been laid to rest – side by side, it had escaped detection for twelve long months until Jack had been able to sneak in and retrieve it.

Twelve months full of sleepless nights; full of yearning and anguish. Always fearing that it would be discovered and never within his grasp again.

He had enveloped the box in black plastic and covered it with bark and twigs to ensure its secrecy.

But, what if the tree has been cut down? What if there's been a fire?

The fears had continued to eat away at him until that day when – disguised as a grieving widow – he had reached into that spider-webbed abyss and touched the bark-encrusted package with his own fingertips.

Jack closed his eyes now and opened the lid. With them still closed, he let his fingers wander to the heavenly contents. There, the silky trophies of his special girls greeted him. Each severed ponytail – gathered and secured with hardened resin.

He lifted them out of the box – one by one. Reliving the thrill of each capture and coupling. Loving each sweet child in his own dark way.

Charity's hair had been long and brown; Amy's a heart-wrenching auburn. He brought the souvenirs to his cheek and then sniffed them greedily. He had already collected seven of different colors and textures, but he still longed for the straight, silky black tresses of an Asian child. Su Lin. Her lips so soft and full; her movements so deliberate and graceful. . .

He had picked her out of the church congregation months ago, and had been watching her comings and goings with fanatical interest. Driving different cars and wearing an assortment of hats, sunglasses, mustaches and wigs, he felt certain that his close observation of the child had gone unnoticed.

Little Su Lin took piano lessons every Monday, after school. On those days, she would not ride the bus home, as usual, but walk, instead, to the home of Lois Blankenship nine blocks away.

Poor child. What if it was raining? Surely somebody would see her and offer the child a ride? Of course, she had been taught never to accept a ride from a stranger... But, what about an offer from a kind benefactor who had earned her trust?

His mouth curled up at the corners and watered with anticipation. Soon. Very soon.

25. CLOSING IN

Officer Gentry was standing by his mailbox with an opened envelope in his hands. He was eagerly scanning the second page of a three-page report that he had requested as a favor from a friend on the force.

It was a background check on one Earnest Gormsley now residing in Charlottesville, VA. The first two pages were disappointing. The man had no criminal record. He had been in trouble several times for hiring illegal immigrants, but many rural farmers were guilty of that offense. The immigrants were willing to work much harder and for much less compensation. And, the economy what it was these days. . .

It was the third page that caused his heart to somersault within the birdcage of his ribs. He hadn't been certain until that very instant that Janice was on the right path.

His hands dropped to his sides and he turned his face heavenward. A hawk was gliding expertly through the blue summer sky; it's wings spread wide as it turned on one breeze, then the next. Mike took in a deep breath and let it out slowly to calm his acrobatic pulse.

Earnest Gormsley died ten years ago. He was only 48 years old at the time of his death. Unmarried.

Mike was suddenly aware that he had to call Janice right away. She needed to stay clear of that man and let the police take over the investigation from here. Could it be true? Could they really have Jack Garrett at their fingertips?

Mike had never been much for church on Sundays, but he had always believed in God. His most fervent prayer had been that he would apprehend Jack Garrett prior to his retirement from the force. Well. Maybe God's timing had been a bit slow, but Mike would take it, and Halleluiah.

With long strides, the former Officer Gentry went to find his wife and his cell phone – whichever came first.

His cell was on the coffee table, first thing he saw as his eyes adjusted to the cool, shadowy interior of his home. It took him a couple of seconds to remember that he hadn't programmed her number into it. With the phone in his hand he loped into the bedroom and cast his eyes about for that slip of paper. The one he had scrawled her number on only a few weeks ago. Nothing on the dresser, the bed-side tables or the chest of drawers...

With growing frustration, he started opening drawers and shifting items off of chairs. Nothing.

"Virginia? Where are you?"

"What? Mike? Are you calling me?"

The faint reply came from the sun porch, so he headed in that direction and met his wife halfway.

"I need to find that yellow piece of paper we wrote Janice's phone number on. It's really important. Do you have any idea what I did with it?"

"Well, yes."

He sighed with relief. "Okay? Where is it?"

"I found it in the pocket of your blue button down when I was doing the laundry and I threw it away."

Mike put his face in his hands and groaned. "Why would you throw it away? Why? Didn't you think I might need to call it sometime?"

Virginia pulled his hands away from his face and planted a kiss on his cheek. "Well, as a matter of fact, the thought did occur to me. That's why I copied it down in our address book."

A slow smile smoothed the lines of his face and he slid his arms around her waist and kissed her full on the lips with all the passion of a much younger man.

"You did! You did! Of course you did! You always do right by me, you lovely, wonderful, thoughtful woman!"

He left her laughing and shaking her head to find the address book that resided in a kitchen drawer along with many random items, such as rubber bands, abandoned twist-ties and loose change.

While waiting for Janice to answer, he lifted the top off of the cookie jar and stole two Oreos. Good news had always sharpened his appetite.

"Hello?"

"Janice? Mike Gentry."

"Oh, Hi Officer Gentry! I'll have what we talked about by Sunday night. Can I drop it by late? Say, 10:00 p.m.?"

"Janice. Whatever you're planning, you need to give it up right now."

He heard her tell someone that she was going to step out back to take the call.

"What? No. You don't understand. I had the greatest idea. . ."

"Janice. I just got the background report on Mr. Gormsley. Are you sitting down, 'cause this is a shocker."

"Not sitting, but I'm ready to hear good news. It *is* good news, right?"

"I guess that depends. Honey, Earnest Gormsley died ten years ago."

"Dead? That makes all kinds of sense, then, doesn't it?"

"Yes. I'm afraid so. I don't know how you did it, but you may have actually found the bastard."

"Like I told you. . ."

"Exactly." He agreed.

"I knew it. Deep down in my bones, I just knew it was him."

He listened closely as she proceeded to fill him in on all that had happened; her job at the diner, the Gormsley playground, her plan to bring him Earnest's prints and DNA as soon as her shift was over on Sunday night.

"It sounds as though he's building a fortress of good will so that he won't fall suspect when children start to go missing."

"Well, it's *working!*" Her exasperation came over the cell waves with diamond clarity.

"Are you at the Diner now?"

"Yes. My shift isn't over until 8:00 p.m."

"Are you sure nobody has overheard you?"

"Yep. I'm out back. Nobody around. No worries."

Mike Gentry took a moment to think. Janice was a bright girl. She had come up with this plan on her own, and it was pretty damn fool proof. But, could he allow her to take the risk?

"Officer Gentry? Are you still there?"

"Yes. Sorry. I was thinking things out a bit."

"So? Do I go ahead with "Operation Dirty Dishes?"

"I'm going to say 'yes,' but it scares me to death."

Janice laughed and, with her usual lightheartedness, she dismissed any risk by saying, "Hey. I'm just the dishwasher. Who suspects the dishwasher?"

"Well, okay. But, I'm driving out there, myself and I'm bringing a gun. Can't send my best detective in without reinforcements."

He hung up with a bad feeling. What would Jack do to anyone who got in his way? It didn't bear thinking about. Virginia came up behind him with a question mark knitted into her brows. He wrapped his arms around his wife and told her the life story of one Earnest Gormsley of Charlottesville, VA.

26. WHO DOES THAT??

Janice was at work bright and early that Sunday. She couldn't see the tables from her place in front of the sink, but she peeked through the round window in the service doors every time the front door chimes announced the arrival of new patrons.

She didn't have to wait long, as the chimes announced the Gormsleys shortly after 7:00 a.m. They were dressed in their finest "go-to-meeting" clothes and wasted no time settling their fine selves into the second booth on the right – Station 9 – that was Christy's section.

Ducking out of sight, Janice had to work to appear nonchalant. Mack had noticed the Gormsley's grand entrance and had pointed it out to Janice along with his usual peppering of local news.

"Let's just see how long Barry holds to his 'free food' promise." He laughed, conspiratorially. He's out there, now – just bowing and scraping like nobody's business. Now, that's something I'd never expected to see in my lifetime."

Janice laughed at the appropriate times, but was too apprehensive about completing her assigned task to hold up her end of the conversation.

"My, but you are quiet this morning. You feeling okay?" She looked up to see him eyeing her with concern.

"Oh. I'm fine." She smiled, widely. "I didn't sleep well last night, that's all. You be sure to wake me up if I fall asleep in the suds, will you?"

Satisfied for the moment, Mack nodded and turned his attention back to the grill. "He gets the pancakes, she gets the French toast and bacon."

"What?"

"Earnest Gormsley never eats ham. Not in this restaurant, anyway. Maybe he gets enough of it at work."

She chimed in "It's probably the slaughtering that takes the joy out of it for him, don't you think? I know if I was killing and carving up animals all day, I'd find it hard to eat them afterward."

"Oh, he doesn't do any of his own slaughtering!"

She turned and met Mack's eyes.

"You look surprised!" He chuckled. "Nope. His hired hands to all the dirty work."

No. He just butchers little girls.

Janice felt a film of sweat forming on her face, scalp and neck. She pictured the farmer's gory jeans and apron and a chill of nausea shook her.

"You okay? You really don't look so good." He said, worried again.

She turned her back to him and busied herself with a stack of dirty plates.

"I'm fine. Really. It is just so hot in here this morning."

Every few minutes, Mack walked over to peek at the couple through the service door window. Janice saw him looking more and more perplexed.

"What's that face all about?"

"What are you saying? Oh. I guess I do look a mite confused, at that."

"Well?" Janice put a sudsy hand on her hip, waiting for an explanation.

"That Earnest Gormsley is just not right in his head."

"I agree with you, for lots of reasons, but. . . "

"Come on over here and watch him eat his food."

"What? Why?" She asked, as she crossed the kitchen to the service door.

What she saw caused her heart to drop. Mr. Gormsley had napkins wrapped around the ends of each utensil. He was drinking his orange juice through a straw.

"Who does that?" Mack asked her, incredulously.

"Apparently, he does."

"Bizarre."

Janice knew that it would only take one fingerprint or one drop of saliva to positively identify him as the murderer that he was. The straw would be sufficient, all by itself. And, prints could be lifted from the table – probably. She thought about the care he had taken to protect the utensils and figured he'd be just as smart about the other surfaces he came into contact with.

Criminy! I can't let him get away. Not without some kind of evidence. Think! Think!

"If I didn't know the good man for the saint that he is, I'd say he had something to hide."

"Hmm?" Janice came out of her reverie.

"I said, only ex-cons worry that much about leaving fingerprints." Mack didn't look happy about his observation.

"Well. I wouldn't worry. Maybe he's just one of those obsessive-compulsive people. You know, worried about flesh-eating bacteria and stuff like that."

Mack seemed to like that explanation. "Yeah. Maybe. But, like I said, he's one strange dude."

An idea occurred to Janice and she turned to Mack with a question.

"Does Barry keep any tape around the Diner?"

"Tape? You mean duct tape? Cellophane tape? Electrical tape?"

"The cellophane type. Actually the wide strips used for closing up boxes and stuff like that would be best."

Mack thought for a minute. "I've never seen any, but, if there is some it would be in the storage room."

Janice looked disappointed again. Barry kept that room locked.

"It's locked, though, isn't it."

"That it is, young lady. That it is."

"What are you needing shipping tape for all of a sudden, anyway?"

She cast about for some kind of plausible explanation. "Um. I bought some fudge from across the street and I want to mail it to my Aunt in Wisconsin for her birthday. I've found a box to put it in, and bought a card, but I need to seal it up before I can take it over to the Post Office."

"Well, then this is your lucky day. Because, I happen to have a key to the storage room in this pocket."

"Really? Can I have it for a minute so I can go look?"

"Here you go. Just don't let the boss catch you in there. Go on in. I'll start whistling if he comes sniffing around."

She grabbed the key and let herself into the storage room. It took her a few minutes to find the light switch as it was behind a stack of boxes. With the light on she could see that finding anything in all of that mess would be quite a feat – let alone a roll of shipping tape.

Finally, Janice emerged from the room with cobwebs in her hair, streaks of dust on her face and uniform, *and* a wide roll of transparent tape.

"You are a mess." Mack said, as he took the key from her and slipped it back into his pocket. He pointed to what was left of his hair and said, "There's stuff all up in there."

Janice combed her fingers through her hair and used the sudsy sink and a rag to clean up a bit.

"I'm going to take my break now, Okay?"

"Go ahead. It's your fifteen minutes. You can take it whenever you want to."

Janice took a generous strip of tape off the roll and let herself out of the kitchen's back door. From there, she walked carefully around to the Diner's parking lot. This would be the dangerous part. She needed to get what she was after without being seen.

The whole front of Barry's Diner was glass. There were no curtains or shades to block the parking lot from view.

Her only saving grace was that Greta was seated to face the lot – not Earnest. Janice took in her surroundings and decided it was now or never.

"Here goes nothing." She said through gritted teeth.

Before she had time to think about the danger she was putting herself in, Janice darted out between the cars and headed for the sleek black Lexus that belonged to the Gormsleys. The Lexus had a keyless entry! Janice was thrilled. The code keypad would be sure to yield useable prints.

Once on the driver's side, she pressed the strip of tape against the keypad and pulled it free. Breathless, she dodged back around the side of the building and tried to slow her stride and her breathing – the tape still stretched carefully between both hands. She had just turned the corner to the comparative safety of the back of the Diner, when Janice was grabbed from behind and an iron hand was clamped down over her mouth.

27. WHAT TO DO ABOUT JANICE

Mike Gentry paced his living room. It was hard to know what to do with this information. Why hadn't he passed it on to the active officers at the local precinct? Was it because he wanted to be the one to solve this case? Did he honestly believe that the officers would blow everything and give Gormsley an opportunity to run? And, how could he justify letting Janice endanger herself for DNA evidence? Shouldn't he be the one to chase it down?

All of these questions had troubled his sleep and stolen his appetite. Virginia was getting worried about him, he could see that. She had made it pretty clear that she thought he should have turned the lead over to the "real" police the minute he had heard what Janice had found.

Several times, he picked up the cell and started to call the precinct, but he still had that nagging feeling that Janice was right. Most officers wouldn't have taken her claims seriously. They would have seen a young woman with an overactive imagination. Wasn't it best to hold off until they had enough evidence to arrest Jack?

The worst thing that could happen would be for a couple of officers to conduct a casual interview with

Gormsley – that would only serve to warn him and give him another chance to disappear.

Jack Garrett was not stupid. But, he was big-time dangerous. What would he do to Janice if he thought she had guessed his true identity? Mike shuddered. He needed to get out there and stop her from carrying out her plan. Even though it had seemed fool proof to him, he couldn't allow Janice to fall prey to somebody like that. Perhaps he could come up with an idea to get the proof they needed?

"Honey?" He called out to the front porch where his wife was watering hanging plants.

"I'll be right in." She called.

Mike Gentry gathered his keys and wallet up off the dresser and changed his plaid shorts for a pair of khakis.

"Mike?"

"I'm here." He ducked out of the bedroom and found her waiting.

"Where are you off to?"

"I've just thought of something that needs doing out Charlotte way."

She looked worried. "Mike. What are you going to do? Please, don't go after that man by yourself. Can't you just send the guys out there? You aren't a policeman anymore. You don't have to take those risks."

"I won't be in any danger. I promise." He cajoled. "I just have to stop Janice from doing anything stupid. I should never have let her go off by herself in the first place."

"Mike. Please."

"Now, Honey. You know Janice is too headstrong for her own good. I just need to talk some sense into her before she gets in over her head. You don't want to see that girl getting hurt, do you?

"Of course, not. . . but,"

"Honey, I will be back in a few hours. I promise."

Virginia didn't look happy about his trip, but she had known him long enough to see that further argument would not move him.

"You be back here for dinner, Mike Gentry. You be back here, or I'll call the police, myself!"

Ex-Officer Gentry laughed and pulled his wife into his arms for a kiss.

"Well, that depends." He joked, "What's for dinner?"

28. RAINY DAYS AND MONDAYS

Earnest greeted Monday morning with a yawn and a stretch. Today would be a very good day. The weatherman was calling for an afternoon thunderstorm, and he was planning to be on "good Samaritan" standby for his favorite girl.

How many times had he seen his sweet and serious Su Lin hiking to her piano class through 100-degree heat or punishing downpours? Couldn't her parents see that she needed a ride? He stepped into the shower and shook his head in disbelief.

That poor child!

If he had a daughter like that – a pretty, pure, innocent daughter, with almond eyes and a serious nature, he would guard her unfailingly! Carry her to her piano lessons like a princess and be there to pick her up when class was over.

The water washed down his body past the new obstacle that had sprung to life as he had lathered himself and pondered Su Lin. He often thought that he should have had children. He would have been a much better parent than these clowns who clearly didn't value their precious little girls. God had given them a sacred stewardship, and they had repeatedly failed to protect Su Lin. He frowned and shook his head.

A picture flashed across his mind of the destroyed and dismembered body of the last one, but he pushed it aside with shock and revulsion. She had been a threat, after all, and threats were not to be tolerated. She had displeased him by putting up a fight and being disrespectful. It would be better with Su Lin. Feeling more optimistic, he put the last experience behind him. Thinking about things like that would just spoil his mood and put a damper on the joy of this new conquest.

As Earnest patted himself dry and contemplated his muscles in the steamed mirror, he could hear Greta stirring from her bedroom down the hall. He was growing increasingly tired of her prattle. If she wasn't a cornerstone of his new identity, he would have put her aside months ago.

The way things stood, however, she was too useful to dispose of. She was hard to ignore – a real presence – and she had been very effective as a deterrent to bothersome neighbors and any who would call themselves "friends." He was thankful that she knew her place and had never shown any interest in sharing his room.

It would be difficult to wait for school to let out. He had to keep telling himself that half the experience was the thrill of anticipation. He imagined holding Su Lin as she trembled and cried to be set free. The way he would gather up her silky hair and use it to drag her and force her into the trunk of whichever car he chose to use for the day's festivities.

He hoped Su Lin would behave herself and refrain from screaming and kicking. It would be unfortunate to be forced to knock her out. But, he felt certain that this child would be appropriately submissive and easily overpowered. That was always best.

Earnest pulled a tee shirt over his head and stepped into a pair of charming overalls. Even though he had very little to do with the operation of the farm, he felt it was important to look the part.

As he padded towards the kitchen, he could smell coffee and toast. His stomach rumbled. It was on days like these that his appetite was always the sharpest. He greeted his hideous wife with a virginal kiss on the cheek and accepted the light breakfast with gratitude – wishing her a good morning.

"And, how did you sleep, my husband?" She asked, sweetly.

"Very well. Very well, thank you."

"Would you like preserves for your toast this morning?"

"Yes. I'll have the Damson Plum that you put up. Yours are always so much better than store bought."

Greta beamed as she broke the seal on a fresh jar and brought it to the table.

"I should show you my appreciation more often, my sweet." He said. "I know! How about a little spa and shopping trip? Would you like that? Perhaps a night out with your sisters? I will pick up the tab."

Her transformation was immediate. Greta liked nothing better than to offer her sisters the benefits of her wealth and high social standing. She was on the phone making plans before he could finish his coffee.

What a good old girl to get the hell out of his way when he had "work" to do.

This was going to be a very good day.

29. GIVE ME THE TAPE

Janice stood still in her captor's grasp. Frozen with terror, her heartbeat seemed louder than the sounds of passing traffic, and she could feel it in her neck and wrists; the frenzied beating of a hummingbird's wings.

"Shhh! Don't scream, Janice. It's me. Officer Gentry. Can I move my hand? Are you going to be okay?"

Janice nodded her head and nearly fainted dead away as he released her. Mike saw that she was unsteady on her feet and moved in to support her.

"You . . ." She fought for breath. "You scared me to death."

"I'm sorry. I didn't catch up to you until you were ready to go inside. I was afraid of startling you and causing a commotion."

She started to relax a bit as understanding dawned on her. "Okay. That was probably a good idea, then. Just don't ever do it again!"

"That's a promise. Give me the tape. Then, you could run back in and bring me a strip of waxed paper to mount it on?"

Janice knew where the butcher paper was kept and nodded in assent. Carefully, she passed the strip to Officer Gentry. They examined it together.

"Did I get anything?"

He smiled. "Yes, ma'am, I think you may have!"

Her face lit up with the hope that gave her.

"I thought you were going to bring me dirty dishes? What happened?"

"He's too smart for that. I'll tell you later. I'll be right back."

Mack watched Janice make a beeline over to the butcher paper and tear off a piece.

"What are you up to now?"

She gave him the universal sign for "Not now!" and scurried back outside holding the scrap carefully – by its edges – so as not to contaminate any prints they may have collected.

Once the strip of tape had been mounted safely on the paper, Officer Gentry patted Janice's shoulder and moved as if to go. Then, at the last minute, he turned back.

"Tell them whatever you need to, and get yourself home! I mean, now!"

"But, I might be able to get some DNA from . . ."

"Janice. We've got it from here. You've done a wonderful thing; a very brave thing. Now, get home. Call me when you get there."

"But. . ."

"I would like to live long enough to enjoy my golden years, Janice Schuster. You seem bound and determined to give me a coronary."

The fight gone out of her, Janice agreed to do as he instructed and waved him off.

Mack greeted her at the door with his hands firmly planted on his hips.

"Are you going to tell me what that was about? Why did that guy tell you to play sick and go home?"

"You really shouldn't be listening at doors, you know. It isn't polite."

"Are you in some kind of trouble, Janice?"

She raised her eyes to his and contemplated telling him everything.

"No. Nothing like that."

"Barry's going to burst a vein if you ask to leave early."

She sighed and shrugged her shoulders.

"Mack. I can't explain what just happened, but we're friends, right?"

He rolled his eyes and raised his hands in defeat.

"Right."

"I need to go home. I'm not feeling well at all."

"You do look a bit green around the gills, now that you mention it." He winked, conspiratorially.

"Will you tell Barry that I'll call him about tomorrow? I'll be in if I'm feeling better. "

"Will you?" His face was all over serious.

She looked at her feet. The answer was no. This would be her last day at Barry's Diner. She would miss his wild stories and updates on all of the town's gossip.

"You're not, are you."

"No, Mack. This is my last day. I'll explain everything as soon as I can. You'll understand. I promise."

He wrapped her up in an unexpected bear hug and told her to "get on home."

"Thanks, Mack." Janice flashed her famous million-dollar smile and pushed her way back through the squeaky screen door.

The Buick waited, faithfully, in the back of the lot. She locked herself in as soon as the door swung shut, and left the windows up until she was safely out of town.

Until Officer Gentry had shown up, she had convinced herself that nothing could go wrong; that she wasn't in any danger. But, she had been given a bad scare when she thought Jack had her in his grasp. The realization that she was safe and free to go home had been all the encouragement she needed.

Janice shuddered. Tears ran down her face, unchecked. They were tears of relief, fear, exhaustion, and sadness. She had done her part. She was going home.

30. IN OUT OF THE RAIN

Earnest had chosen his '64 Pontiac Catalina for the day's festivities. It had taken a while to extricate it from the weeds and rusting hulks where it had been concealed for months.

As he knew it would, the engine turned over like a champ on the first try. A light rain pattered against the windshield and the roof; a puff of exhaust wove its way through those droplets with sinuous elegance, and the rumble and bounce of his drive to the outbuildings added horsepower to the level of his exhilaration. Soon, he would be back here with a plaything in the trunk. There were preparations to be made.

Earnest Gormsley melted away with the completion of each task and he found himself moving and thinking like Jack Garrett, "The Shortcut Stalker." The smile that helped to complete that transformation was chilling; ruthless, eager, even gleeful.

Jack removed the padlock and entered his private "workshop." To the right he pulled a string to add a circle of yellowed light to his activities. A battered green footlocker held a selection of license plates. Two had already been set aside. Jack grabbed the next in line and pulled a screwdriver out of his toolbox.

Once the license plate had been affixed, Jack lifted a cardboard box containing a pair of brand-new moving quilts, some zip ties and a roll of duct tape. The trunk slammed shut with a satisfying thud that aroused him.

Soon. Very soon.

A turn of the wrist told him it was 2:30 already. School would be letting out. His plan was to intercept her in the middle of her journey where the area became more rural and the average age of the homeowners was 65. Su Lin would be walking alone through a downpour – already soaked through -- when he appeared to offer her a ride.

There were no words to describe the thrill that this thought gave him. He would have her all to himself until that moment when he would have to watch her go. The dimming of her eyes, the stillness in her limbs. . .

But, Jack wasn't about to ruin these precious hours with thoughts of the sad and messy work that would follow. All images of rot and ruin were pushed from his mind and locked away with whatever had been left of his humanity.

He glided past the school like a great white shark. Knowing it was there, but acknowledging it only as a landmark on his journey. Little girls climbed aboard buses and into their parent's cars to go home. But, not Su Lin; not today; not ever again.

The road wound delightfully downhill with tidy houses and mature trees huddling against the downpour on either side. With a rush of adrenaline Jack caught his first glimpse of Su Lin -- the poor darling – all alone in the rain with several blocks to go. How happy she would be to see him! How nice it would be to get in out of the rain!

The Catalina pulled up ahead of her and stopped. Jack reached over to roll down the passenger-side window.

"Su Lin! Su Lin? Isn't that your name?"

The little girl stopped and bent over to see who was calling her name.

"Hi! Remember me? I go to your church. I am the guy who put the playground in at the Elementary school?"

She looked again, and he could see the light of recognition switch on behind her eyes.

"Do you need a ride somewhere? I hate to see you out on a day like this."

Su Lin hesitated. She started to refuse his offer, but changed her mind at the last minute and climbed in beside him.

"Where can I drop you off?"

Jack pretended to listen as she gave directions and continued towards the house of Su Lin's piano teacher.

"Could you wind that window up, Hon? It will be a lot dryer that way." This with his warmest, most sincere, fellow church member smile.

An obedient child, she immediately did as she was asked.

"You are soaked through." He observed.

"Yes."

"Here let me dry your face." He made as if to dab at her face with a pink and white towel that had been resting on the seat next to him, but instead had clamped the ether-soaked cloth over her nose and mouth until the child went limp.

Jack cruised past the piano teacher's house and continued on until he reached a quiet court that was ringed with empty lots. It was easy to shift the sweet child into the trunk, press duct tape over her mouth, zip tie her hands and feet, and wrap her up gently inside the moving quilts.

The storm intensified, even as he closed the trunk lid, and he stood behind the car for a few extra moments to feel the cleansing barrage of water on his face. He had wanted the rain, and the rain had come. In his mind, the child was meant to be his. And she was.

31. BILLY MEETS A GIRL

Billy Fische was sleeping soundly after a hectic day. A silver thread of drool connected his face to the pillow, and a gentle snoring drifted rhythmically through the room. Through the window shone one faint beam of moonlight, and in that beam, a shape began to take form.

At first, there was only a misty pair of legs. Those were followed shortly thereafter by a torso and arms. If he had been watching, Billy would have begun to question why she was headless. But, after several moments, a head did begin to form. Very gradually, the details began to fill in; red gym shorts and a red and white striped shirt. Long blonde hair that was parted on the side and fell over half of her face to cascade over one shoulder.

Billy felt someone sit on the bed and a small hand on his shoulder began to shake him into wakefulness. In the time it took to become fully conscious he had ascertained that his visitor was not of the living variety.

"Who's here?" He asked, tentatively. Then, he saw her. "Hello?"

"Help her." The little spirit said, plaintively. "He took me, and he has taken her."

"Who? Who has taken who? (or whom?)" Billy shook his head, deciding it was much too early for proper grammar rules to apply.

"Do you know Janice?"

"What?"

"Find Janice. Help her."

"Janice? What? Janice who?"

The little spirit faded away just as gradually as it had arrived.

"Do you mean *Janice Schuster?*"

The room was empty again. The beam of moonlight, now unoccupied.

Billy propped up his pillows and tried to put the pieces of the conversation together. What had she said? Something about "He has taken me and . . . "

There was, of course, the outside possibility that this visitation had been a figment of his imagination. But why would he imagine a little girl asking for help? And, Janice Schuster? He hadn't thought about her in years."

He switched on his bedside lamp and the thought that flooded into him along with the yellowed light caused his heart to thump and his breathing to accelerate.

Jack Garrett. She was talking about Jack Garrett. He took her, and he has taken another. . . Janice."

Billy grabbed his alarm clock and fought the idea that calling anybody at 2:00 a.m. would be out of the question. But, he couldn't put aside the urgency in the little girl's plea. In moments, he had secured the Schuster's phone number from information and begun to dial. If he was right, Janice would understand. She would want him to call right away. Wouldn't she?

"Janice?" he asked the sleepy girl who answered the phone. "This is Billy Fische. I'm sorry to call so late. You aren't going to believe what just happened to me."

32. A VOICE IN THE NIGHT

Janice was having a nightmare. Spent from all of her efforts in Charlottesville, she had fallen into bed upon her return home on Sunday and had hardly stirred.

In her nightmare, Janice was grabbed from behind on the trail in Harlan's woods. The surrounding trees had been black and full of malice, alive somehow, and were curling their roots up to trip her at every opportunity. When the hand of her assailant came away from her mouth, she screamed. But instead of an earsplitting plea for help, there was only the plaintive cawing of a crow.

Then, bound hand and foot, she was given to the twisted limbs of the largest, most menacing tree, to be lifted up and up and up until any fumble would mean instant death. Filled with terror, Janice cawed again and again. The branches scraped and cut at her arms and legs as they continued to bear her higher and higher.

Then, the boughs released her. Janice fell. The grasping branches had simply loosened their hold on her and down she went; down and down. The sky was purple and blue and green and yellow; a bruise, she thought – just like a bruise, anyway. The falling seemed to go on and on, until she began to wish for the end with all of her heart – just so that it could be over.

It was then that great black wings opened up from somewhere behind her shoulder blades. They stretched out from her sides, and the stretching felt wonderful. She wasn't falling anymore. Her fear was replaced with a feeling of strength that she wouldn't have believed possible, and she laughed as she put Harlan's woods and its dark inhabitants far behind her.

Somewhere, a song was playing. . . A song that she knew. . . A song. . .

Janice sat up in bed. Her cell was ringing out some jazzy tune that she had picked out of a ring tone menu months before and could no longer stand.

"Hello?"

"Janice?"

"This is she. Her. It's Janice." She yawned and stretched.

"This is Billy Fische. I'm sorry to call so late. You aren't going to believe what just happened to me."

Janice listened to his story with rapt attention. "She said Jack has another child? Now?"

It took only a few minutes to fill Billy in on all that had been happening, and how they all believed that Jack had come back, and that they were on the verge of nabbing him. "The little ghost. . . what did she look like?"

"She was around seven or eight years old, long blonde hair. She was wearing red shorts and a kind-of striped top. . ."

"Oh my God." Janice breathed.

"That's Cherie. She has been missing for a couple of weeks."

"Well, I don't know how she knew to look me up, but she was positively determined that I should get your attention."

"And, what exactly did she say?"

"She said that he had taken her and was taking another kid. She seemed to think that you could help the latest victim."

"Billy, I have to make some calls. You did the right thing. I'll do my best."

"Will you call and let me know what's going on?"

"Yes. I'll call you right away when I find out more."

After hanging up, Janice rang Officer Gentry's cell. She knew it was too early. He must have turned the ringer off, because his voicemail picked up.

"Officer Gentry? It's Janice. Don't ask me how I know, but Jack has just picked up another little girl. We have to move fast! Call me. Call me as soon as you get this."

33. THANK GOD FOR AFIS

The retired officer stood behind his partner of eleven years; eyes riveted to a computer screen that was rolling through fingerprints like some kind of futuristic slot machine. Ben had agreed to take the print evidence from Mike and run it through AFIS (otherwise known as the "Automated Fingerprint Identification System"). Janice had managed to lift two clear prints from Gormley's Lexis, as well as a partial thumbprint. Now, all they had to do was match them to Garrett.

"You really think this is the guy?" Ben asked, doubtfully.

"Well, if he isn't, he should be. The real Earnest Gormsley died ten years ago."

"You're shitting me."

"Not at all. At the very least, this guy is going up for identity theft."

Long minutes ticked by as they stared at the screen. Mike Gentry's right foot was tapping, and he smoothed his hair back every couple of minutes. In between the tapping and the smoothing there were heavy sighs. The wait seemed interminable.

"If this is really Jack Garrett, we ought to offer that young woman a spot on the force." He joked.

"She's a natural detective, Ben. You could do a lot worse."

Their conversation was interrupted by an irritating tone from the computer. The screen was flashing. They had a match.

"Damn if you haven't got Jack M.F. Garrett! How the hell did you guys ever find him? I don't fricking believe this!"

Mike sunk to a nearby chair and put his head in his hands. He fought back the tears that pricked his eyes, and tried to get a grip on the trembling in his arms and legs. Anyone would have thought they were tears of happiness, but they were actually born of relief. He had carried the burden of Jack's escape for so many years that having it lifted from his shoulders brought him down like a house of cards.

We've got him. We've finally got him. I've got to call Janice. I've got to call my wife. Oh, thank God in heaven. We're going to put him on death row and watch him rot.

"You okay, Mike?" Ben's hand was on his shoulder.

Mike nodded – his head still cradled in his hands.

One by one, as news spread around the precinct, the officers came to congratulate him. The celebratory atmosphere and camaraderie had been sorely missed over the last few months, and it was hard to break free to contact Janice and Virginia.

"Fact is, we haven't got him until we've got him." The Sergeant's voice boomed from the doorway. "How about less celebrating and more strategizing, boys?"

Mike was in instant agreement.

"I think we should call in the Feds for this one."

The room went silent. All eyes were on Mike.

"Look guys, this man is capable of anything. He slipped our nets the last time, and he'll do it again. We owe it to the little girls who might be his next victims to send out the big guns."

Frank Evans was dumbfounded. "I can't believe you are standing there telling us to call in the Feds! The dude doesn't expect us, he's a sitting duck on a hog farm, for Christ's sake! What makes you think we aren't capable of bringing him in?"

"I agree with them, Mike." Ben spoke up. "Why should the Feds get all the glory, when it was one of our guys who solved the case?"

"Look, everybody." Ex-Officer Gentry lifted his hands in a posture of surrender. "I understand where you're coming from. Glory, fame and all that. You need to get him under 24-hour surveillance right now. I don't need to tell you that we need to be invisible, right? We don't need to tip him off. Once the Feds have positioned themselves, road blocks should go up and an impenetrable perimeter should be established – with as many of our men as the Sergeant here can deploy. I'm just asking you to put the lives of every little girl within 100 miles of that sick bastard ahead of your egos, and let the big guys bring him in."

There was a murmur of protest, but the power of Mike's raised voice squashed all dissent and restored silence to the squad room.

"Contact Agents Trask and Harter. They took over the case from us ten years ago. They want this guy just as badly as we do. Let's all work together and bring this bastard in."

Ben's voice could be heard on a nearby extension.

"Hello. I'd like to speak with Agent Trask or Agent Harter, please. This is the Fredericksburg Police Department. We have a lead on one of their cold cases. Yes. Thanks. I'll hold."

Officer Gentry reached for his cell to call Janice and saw that he had messages. His smile at hearing Janice's voice turned to concern as he listened to what she had to say.

Another child? How could she know that? He ignored the hubbub of the officers around him and dialed her number.

"Hi. Mike Gentry. I just got your message. What in the blue blazes are you talking about?"

"Don't ask. Okay? Just don't ask. You've believed me up till now, right?"

"Well, regardless of all that, I've got good news for you, Janice Schuster."

"We got a match?"

"We got a match!"

"YES!" Janice yelled this so loudly that he had to move the phone away from his ear.

"What are we going to do now? Do the police know? The FBI?"

"Everybody's on board. Our plan is to move in on him tonight."

Janice had to stop and think what day it was.

"Tonight? Why not right now?"

"Calm down. It takes a few hours to get everybody into position and all of the warrants signed, etc. Nobody is going to tip him off. We'll have him in a cell by tomorrow morning, and on death row as soon as humanly possible." She could hear the smile in his voice

"Well, it can't be soon enough. Can you check to see if there have been any children reported missing in the last day or two? If he's got her, then you're going to have to be careful about how you guys approach him."

"Okay. It can't hurt to check. Someday, though, you're going to have to tell me how you know all of this stuff."

"Just hurry, okay? This little girl needs help – fast."

"Janice?"

"Yes?"

"I want you to pursue a career in law enforcement. Would you think about doing that? I happen to know a police sergeant who will be standing by to give you a job."

Janice fell back onto her pillows. "You know what, Officer Gentry? I don't think that's a half-bad idea."

"Okay. Well, they won't let me anywhere near Charlottesville tonight, so I'm going to be waiting for the news just like everybody else. If you hear something first, call me!"

"Ditto."

"You did an amazing thing, Janice. Charity would have been so proud of you." There was a pause. "I am so proud of you."

"Thanks. Can I be proud of me too?"

They both laughed, and when the call ended, she jumped into the shower and sang top 40 hits with all the wrong lyrics. They had him. The little girl would be saved and Jack Garrett was going to be eating crow on death row before the sun could rise again.

A career in law enforcement? Detective Janice Shuster.
It did have a certain ring to it.

But, somewhere in the shadows of her confidence there crouched a black hearted Beast of Doubt.

What if. . . ?

34. THE SHED

Su Lin awoke to darkness and the smells of mold and earth and hay. Her wrists and ankles were bound painfully with plastic ties, but after struggling for several minutes, she had been able to sit up and look around. The building was made of old, graying boards. It must be dark outside, because tiny gaps between the boards would have given her more light to examine her surroundings.

She had almost refused the offer of a ride. A polite, "No, thank you, Mr. Gormsley," had been knocking on her teeth, but the rain. . .

Her mother would be very angry. She knew better than to get into a car with anybody. But, Mr. Gormsley? He was in their church – not a stranger. He had built the playground for the little kids. Everybody said he was a great guy. . .

A movement startled her, and she tried to see what had made the noise. A field mouse ran across her foot, and she relaxed. She wasn't afraid of a little mouse. Then there was another sound from the far corner.

A snake? Could there be snakes in here?

Su Lin wanted to cry, but her head was hurting very badly, and she felt like she might throw up. The ties on her wrists and ankles were cutting into her skin and had started to bleed in places.

As her eyes became accustomed to the darkness, she began to make out shapes; a shovel, a pitchfork, a table in the center of the room with . . . with. . .

No. No. No.

There was a butcher's blade hanging from a nail on one end of the table. It had a nasty look about it. She knew it was meant to cut up her body into parts. Su Lin needed to get out of there. Could she stand up?

She pushed her back up against the wall of the shed and pushed upwards with her feet. This caused her ankles to sting with pain, but Su Lin did her best to ignore it. Within minutes, she was standing.

She hopped to the corner of the table where the butcher's blade hung. Hopping around until her back was to it, she forced her hands to lift it off of the nail. It took several attempts to get the knife free, but, when she did, she nearly cried out with relief.

There was a workbench on the far end of the shed. She could barely make out the tools that were hanging on the wall behind it.

Maybe there is something over there I can use to hold the blade so I can cut my hands free?

Carefully, slowly, Su Lin hopped towards the workbench. She had almost crossed the room when she landed on something sharp and horrible. She did cry out, then. And, though she tried to stay upright, the shock and pain of the injury had caused her to fall – face first – onto the cement floor.

She heard the sickening crunch of her nose breaking before she could feel the pain. Crying, she rolled onto her back and swallowed so much blood that she was sure she was dying.

"You are never to give up! We are strong in this family, Su Lin. We keep at it until we get it right. Now, get to work! Show them all that Su Lin can do anything they can do! Su Lin can do it better!"

Her Grandfather's words came to her from out of nowhere. His voice was firm. Su Lin knew that her Grandfather had been dead for many years, but she heard him, just the same. While on her back, she bent her knees and pushed hard against her feet. In this way, she gradually made her way to the workbench and was able to press her back against one of its sturdy supports and stand.

As she had hoped, there was a vice grip attached to the bench a few feet to her left. She knew that her feet were cut and bleeding. The pain was sharp and hard to ignore, but she worked her way down to the vice and struggled with it until she had affixed the horrible butcher's blade firmly within its grasp.

A faint glimmer of hope lit up her heart and some tears started to fall down her ruined face. The blade was sharp and her hands came free almost as soon as the ties made contact with it.

Her face was pounding at the rate of her pulse, and she could feel her eyes beginning to swell shut. Her breath was coming faster as she loosened the butcher knife from the grip and cut the ties at her ankles. There was an instant lessening of pain when the ties let go of her.

Su Lin was unbound and armed, but she needed to find a way out. The blood was dripping off of her chin, and she was finding it harder and harder to see as her eyelids continued to swell.

She moved along the wall searching for an opening of any kind. At last, she believed she had found a pair of large, double doors. Like the doors on a barn. Pushing on them as hard as she could proved what she had thought all along. The doors were securely locked from the outside. There was no way out.

Pieces of sharp straw found their way into her damaged feet, and the pain was almost more than she could bear. Her throat stung with the swallowed blood and her mouth was coppery and dry. She wanted something to drink. Anything.

Grampa? Grampa? Please come back. I am not strong! I am a little girl! I hurt, Grampa. Please. Please. Send someone to help me!

From the blackness Su Lin heard a tiny voice.

"I am here. Help is coming."

Su Lin strained her eyes in the direction the voice had come from. At first, there was nothing – only the unrelenting blackness of her prison. Then, a girl her age was standing there. She had long blonde hair. Su Lin realized that she could see right through her. A ghost?

"Who are you? Can you help me get out of here?"

"I was here before you." The answer was barely audible.

"Did he. . . Did you. . . "

"I never made it out, but you will. "

"Help me! How? How do I get out of here?"

"They are coming to save you. Stay alive. Don't give up. Stay alive."

The spirit faded away to nothing and Su Lin hated that feeling of isolation. She pressed her back against the wall of the shed and clutched the butcher's knife with all of her remaining strength; waiting for whatever was to come.

35. CLOSING IN

The FBI had taken over the Dairy farm that was located just adjacent to Jack Garrett's property. Officers had been mobilized from Charlottesville and Fredericksburg in an unprecedented effort to capture this serial murderer and put him safely behind bars. Of course, if Garrett resisted arrest - - well, anything could happen. There were plenty of men in that group that would have been pleased as punch to put an end to Jack with a well-placed shot to the head, but one thing was certain – there would be no escape.

Mike Gentry had followed Janice's direction, and found that there was a young girl missing. There wasn't much doubt among the officers as to what had happened to her. All they could hope was that the little girl, Su Lin, was still alive and unharmed.

S.W.A.T. was standing by to move in before dawn. They had instructions to spare Greta Gormsley, if possible, as she wasn't considered a suspect. She was believed by most to be simply an unwitting accessory to his disguise.

A helicopter was primed and ready to join in the hunt, should Garrett manage somehow to slip their noose again. Nothing was being left to chance this time.

In spite of Ex-Officer Gentry's belief that he would be barred from this operation, he had been asked to participate as an "observer." He supposed that there were enough officers involved who could sympathize with his strong desire to be there at the end of it all.

Mike looked at his watch. Just after midnight. He ran his hand through his hair for the tenth time in a minute and sat down just long enough to stand up again. It was hard to wait. What if the child was being murdered right that minute? The mobilization seemed to be taking an eternity.

He pulled out his cell and called Janice.

She sounded wide awake. "Got him?"

"No. I wish you could see the show, though. Janice, we've got at least 100 officers here that I can see. That's not to mention the S.W.A.T. guys who are probably invisible to the naked eye by now."

"Did you check to see if anyone. . . "

"Yes. That's why I'm calling. A little girl was taken on her way to piano lesson yesterday."

"Yesterday?" He could hear her draw in a long breath.

"Any chance she's still alive?"

"We think so. We hope so."

"When are you guys going in?"

"Oh. Jeez. I don't know. If it was left up to me, I'd have been down that dirt road an hour ago."

"Can't you hurry them up? Don't they know there's a little girl's life hanging in the balance?"

She sounded to Mike as though she were on the verge of tears.

"They want to be sure they get him, that's all. It will happen soon."

There was a long pause. Mike Gentry ran his hand through his hair.

"Janice?"

"Yes?"

"How did you know?"

"Officer Gentry, do you believe in ghosts?"

"No."

"Okay. Then I won't tell you how I knew."

His brows came together with impatience. "You aren't going to try to tell me that. . ."

"Nope. I'm not going to tell you that the ghost of Cherie DeLapis visited Bill Fische."

"What? Billy? Charity's brother?"

"And I'm not certainly not going to tell you that Cherie sent a message to me through Billy. . . "

He looked over his shoulder as the noise level of the room raised suddenly.

"Janice, I have to go. I think things are getting ready to go down here."

"Call me, if. . ."

"I will. First thing."

He ended the call to see groups of officers leaving the house to occupy their assigned stations. Operation "Get That God Damned Mother Fucker" had finally begun.

36. THE PADLOCK

Su Lin had lost too much blood to remain standing. Instead, she found a dark space under the workbench to huddle and had pulled some of the larger items around to conceal her position. Her efforts to free herself had been painful and exhausting. Her eyes kept wanting to close.

Just a few minutes. I need to sleep. I need to rest for the next part. He is coming to get me. I know he is...

But, just as she was beginning to fall asleep, she heard the scrape of gravel caused by an approaching car. Light from car's headlights came streaming through the cracks in the door.

Su Lin got a firm grasp of the butcher's knife and made herself as small as possible. It was hard to breathe quietly through the mess her face had become, but the bleeding had slowed considerably, and she resigned herself to be quiet – even if she had to hold her breath!

- The car door shut with the kind of heavy thump only an antique car can make.

It's him. He's coming for me.

The little ghost's words echoed in her ears. "They are coming. Stay alive. Stay alive."

Just knowing that help was on its way gave her some measure of courage. Then, she jumped at the loud rattle of the padlock against its brackets. She could hear his breathing through the slats.

He is coming for me. He is coming. He is coming.

Su Lin imagined burying the cleaver deep into his thigh. She would be able to do it. She was strong. She knew there wouldn't be two chances. She would have to cut him so deeply that he would be unable to stop her from getting away.

I'm a Lin. We are strong. We don't stop. We never give up. Stay alive. Stay alive. Help is coming. Stay alive.

The large doors swung wide and the light from his headlights filled the shed. To Su Lin, it was as bright as day, but she knew that his eyes had not had time to adjust to the darkness. She couldn't see him. She could tell by his movements that he was wondering where she had gone. Then, he must have seen one of the severed ties on the ground.

He laughed. It was a terrible laugh. His laugh said that there was no escape from this place. That he thought she was awfully cute for trying, but. . .

"Su Lin? Where are you, little one? I should have known you were smarter than the others. I should have seen it on your face. Su Lin's serious little face."

She could hear him moving away from her to the far end of the shed. Things were being moved and shifted.

"Where are you, honey? There's no point in hiding, you know. We are too far away from anywhere for you to get away. And, I have dogs. Dogs can find little girls very quickly, did you know that?"

She wanted to crawl free of her hiding place and run, but she stayed put. Her plan was to injure him. Injure him badly, so that she would have time to run.

How can I run? My feet are sliced through to the bone and bleeding. Am I going to crawl from here?

"Come on, Su Lin." He said with an eerily friendly voice. "I just want to play with you for a while. Then, I promise I'll make it quick. You won't hurt a bit."

As he moved closer and closer to where she was hiding, Su Lin did her best to hold her breath and be very still.

Soon. Be ready. Soon. You have to get him. Get him deeply. You can't miss.

Before she knew what was happening, the items in front of her began to be pulled aside. She saw his hands as they gripped each box and crate to expose her.

It was his face that loomed in front of her first. His legs were not within range of her weapon. Yet, without hesitation, Su Lin sank the cleaver into his neck with all of the strength that was left to her.

There was blood. So much blood. He reeled back and landed on his backside where he grasped the handle of the blade and tried to pull it free.

After the first shock had passed, Su Lin forgot about his gaping injury and used this time to scramble free and run.

She ran. The pain screamed around her and through her like an electrical current. It was bright and sharp and alive. But the voice had said, "They are coming. Stay alive. Stay alive. Stay alive." So she ran.

37. A LITTLE CHILD SHALL LEAD

The S.W.A.T. team was sent in first. They moved silently towards the farmhouse down the long dirt road, equipped with enough fire power to bring down an army of "Greys" and their mother ship. Not a pebble was displaced as a result of their passage. The total lack of street lights helped to blanket them in darkness.

Already, officers were active setting up road blocks and were in position to create an iron-clad perimeter around the hog farm. Jack Garrett's life on the run was coming to an end. Any attempt he made to resist capture would cost him, dearly.

Those who didn't have daughters on the force, had nieces or sisters. This guy had a neon target on his midsection. Nobody really wanted to trust him to the legal system.

Within 10 minutes, his house was surrounded. The signal was given and they moved as one to enter the house and subdue their quarry. Doors were rammed open in the front and back of the farmhouse. Windows were smashed and entered. Room by room, the S.W.A.T. team cleared. The house was empty.

Craig Lawson radioed central operations and reported their findings with disappointment. The team received orders to search all of the outbuildings – and fast. They were to shoot anything that moved and ask questions later.

Officer Lawson divided his 8-member team into two groups and sent them off to examine the barns and the shed. One, by one they vanished into the night – as only S.W.A.T. can do.

Minutes later, shots were heard, and everyone headed for the old shed. When Craig Lawson arrived at the scene of the conflict, what he saw amazed and sickened him. The men were huddled around a bloody and injured child. Her little face was smashed in and covered in dried blood, her feet had been mutilated, and her wrists and ankles resembled raw meat. One of the men was trying desperately to resuscitate her.

Officer Lang sat behind them on the ground with his head in his hands. "I saw something crawling through the weeds. I thought it was Garrett. I . . ."

Craig got on his radio. "We've found Su Lin. She's been shot. She's not breathing on her own. We need an ambulance."

A cry of dismay went up and the ambulance that had been standing by flew down the pitted dirt road to save Su Lin.

"Have you located Garrett?"

"No. Officer Lawson, replied. No."

Lawson snapped back into his role as team leader and waved his men on towards the shed. There was an old Pontiac parked in front of it with its lights on. As the officers approached, they were aware of an ominous silence. It's doors were hanging open like the maw of a conquered beast.

They entered using standard procedure, but soon found that all of those efforts had been for nothing. There, on the filthy floor, lay an old man in a pool of blood with a meat cleaver buried to the bone in his neck. They looked at each other in silence; every one of them thinking the same thing. Su Lin?

How could such a tiny little girl have killed this monster in one stroke? And, she had been tortured, broken, bloodied when she did it. . .

In the silence that ensued, one voice could be heard radioing central.

"Suspect is deceased. Send in the medical examiner."

"What happened down there? Lawson? Was he a suicide?"

"I'm coming up, Sir. You can debrief me in person."

"The girl?" Lawson asked his radio, hopefully.

"No news, I'm afraid. She wasn't breathing on her own, the last I heard; doesn't look good."

The defeat in their respective voices was plain. It was over, but not for the parents of Su Lin. She had risen like Goliath to slay the monster, only to be shot by those who had come to her rescue.

38. STAYING ALIVE

Su Lin sat next to her body in the ambulance. She thought that it looked pretty gross with its nose all flattened to one side and blood caked in its hair and on its clothes. She kept reaching up to touch her spirit face, and was glad to find her nose upright and centered – the way it was supposed to be. She had been in pain for so many hours that being a spirit came as quite a relief.

I was strong. I killed him, Grampa. I didn't give up.

Then, as if he had heard her thoughts, he was there. Her Grampa. They both smiled to see each other. He was sitting on one side of her body and she was sitting on the other, so they didn't hug, though she knew they both wanted to.

"Su Lin. You were strong, but you have given up!"

"No, Grampa. I killed the monster. I saw him and he was dead!"

"Yes. But, so are you, child. Look at your body lying there on that gurney. You stopped fighting just when it mattered the most!"

Su Lin hung her head. "But, I was hurting, and now I'm not. I was strong."

"In order to beat him, you have to live, Su Lin. You have to go back into your body and live a long life. That is how you will conquer that man."

She looked at her broken body. One bullet had gone into her ribcage on the left side, the other had splintered her left shoulder. She hadn't been able to breathe, and it had hurt so badly. She didn't want to go back.

"Su Lin. You must go back. You must be strong and brave. It is not time for you to die."

She nodded, reluctantly.

"I am brave. I will go back. But, someday, after I live a very long life, I will come to find you, and you will be there."

He smiled the way she remembered.

"Yes. I will be there. I promise. And, I will be very proud."

She met his eyes and steeled herself for the pain. Su Lin climbed back into her broken body, and everything around her lit up and started to beep.

Kaye Giuliani lives with her husband in Maryland. She is the Founder of *Proof Finders Paranormal Investigations* in Odenton, Maryland (www.prooffindersparanormal.com). A cancer survivor of three years, Kaye is chasing her dreams down – one at a time. If you enjoy this book, please "Like" it on Facebook or write a favorable review at Amazon.com.

Made in the USA
San Bernardino, CA
16 September 2014